Flames In The Fire

Lillith Mykals Kennedy

Published by Lillith Mykals Kennedy, 2021.

This is a work of fiction. Similarities to real people, places, or events are entirely coincidental.

FLAMES IN THE FIRE

First edition. June 21, 2021.

ISBN: 979-8201425760

Written by Lillith Mykals Kennedy.

Flames In The Fire
Lillith Mykals Kennedy

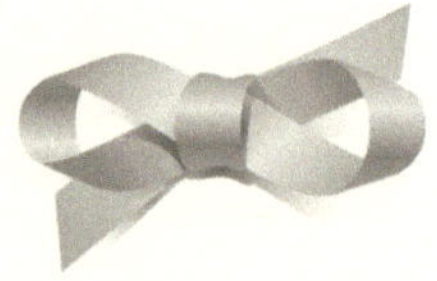

Chapter One

John POV

"You are not listening to me, John. Ellie is sick. She is too sick for you to take home. It would be best if you put her in a long-term care facility. She needs round-the-clock care until she dies," Dr. Joshua Newbern says to me sternly.

I look over the wall of awards. He probably knows more than I do, but I know my wife, and I will be damned if I put her in a hospital to die alone.

"I said I am taking her home with me," I say.

Josh stares at me. I think he is stunned that I am refusing to do what he wants. "Listen, John; I have known you and Ellie for twenty years. I mean, we all went to high school together. I remember the day you two got together like it was yesterday. I have been here every step of the way for her. So I am begging you to listen to me," Josh pleads with me.

I shake my head. "I am taking her home, Josh, and that is final. That is what she wants to do, and that is what we are going to do," I say.

"She will not live long outside the hospital, and you know that, right? So will she consider staying a few more weeks?" Josh asks me.

"Ellie is headstrong and a fighter. You have no idea what she is capable of, and neither do I. She wants to go home, and that is what we are going to do. Please make the arrangements and discharge her," I say.

Josh takes a deep breath. "You will need home health, a nurse around the clock, and someone to sit with her. She cannot be left alone. How are you going to do this and be a cop?" Josh says.

"I will figure it out. I will hire someone to stay with her. My insurance will pay for a nurse. We will work it out," I say.

"John, I understand why, but I do not agree with it," Josh says.

"No, you do not understand. Your wife is healthy. My wife is dying. She is a beautiful young woman, and she is going to die. I want her to die where she wants to die and not in some damn hospital or long-term care facility with people she does not know. Ellie wants to go home, and I will make her last days perfect," I say.

Josh starts scribbling on papers. "I will write the orders for everything she needs. But, John, if it gets bad, I want you to call me immediately, and I will come to her," Josh says.

"Thank you for everything you have done for Ellie," I say. "Everybody loves Ellie. There are a lot of people who will help you with her. But, unfortunately, I do not see her living long outside of the hospital, and there are no treatments left for her," Josh says. "I understand perfectly. It is what she wants," I say.

I walk out of his office and down the hall. I take the elevator up to the fifth floor. I want to cry, but I cannot right now. I have to have my brave face on when I see Ellie. I get off the elevator and walk to her room. When I reach room 5523, I take a deep breath and then go into the room. Ellie looks up and smiles at me when I walk into the room.

"Is Josh going to let me leave this horrible place?" Ellie asks.

I sit down on the side of the bed. "Of course, he is going to let you leave. We are going home as soon as he writes all the orders for you," I say.

Ellie touches my face and smiles. "Thank you for not making me stay here, John. I want to go home and see my animals," Ellie says.

"Oh, I thought you wanted to go home to be with me," I say to her.

"Yeah, I guess you are a bonus. I need you too, but you don't have a fur coat or a wet nose," Ellie says.

I have always said she loved her animals more than me. I know she misses all of them. Her rescue dogs and cats mean the world to her. She has been in the hospital for three weeks this time. Her best friend comes over every day to help feed them while I am at work. Ellie has the heart of a saint. I think that is why I do not understand why someone so special has to be so sick.

The nurse knocks on the door. "Mrs. Daniela Bradley, I have your meds," she says. "Ellie, please, it is Ellie," she says softly. "Sorry, Ellie, I have your meds. Dr. Newbern will be by with your prescriptions to take home and your orders," the young nurse says. "Thank you," I say to her.

Ellie takes her meds. I sit on the side of the bed. I know she will be sleeping soon. The pain medicine always knocks her out. She hates it, but without it, she does nothing but screams. It is unfair for someone who could dance the night away to be confined to a wheelchair. She cannot walk anymore. She cannot brush her hair without half of it falling out. I look down at her nails. Her nails were painted every day, and now they are brittle and cracked. Her beautiful glowing skin is replaced with scales from the treatments. No matter how she looks to everyone else, to me, she is the most beautiful woman on earth.

Ellie reaches out to hold my hand. "I love you almost as much as my animals, John," Ellie says with a smile on her face. I laugh. "I love you too," I say. I hold her hand until she falls asleep. I need to make some calls to get the house ready for her. Her health has deteriorated so much over the last three weeks we will need a hospital bed and a shower chair. I need a nurse for when I work to stay with her. I will give her everything she needs to live out the remainder of her life in our home. I want to make sure she has everything she needs.

I kiss her on the forehead. I love you always, my Ellie.

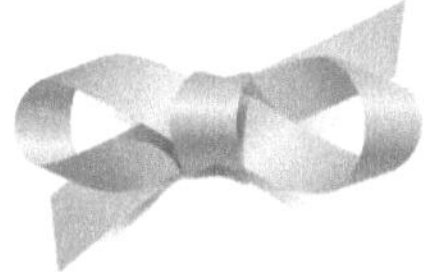

Chapter Two

John POV

I sit on the side of the hospital bed, watching the most beautiful creature I know to sleep soundly from her pain med. I would give anything to take the pain from her. Why couldn't it be me sick? She does not deserve to be lying here in this cold hospital. Soon, my Ellie, I am taking you home today, my love.

FLASHBACK

Noah and I sit at the bar. How in the hell I let him talk me into coming to his sister's wedding. I do not want to be here. Jana and I broke up last week, and I do not want to be around anyone. I want to be at home alone, mad at the world.

"Have a drink," Noah says, handing me a shot.

"Really, you want to get me drunk?" I ask him.

"If you are going to be a sourpuss all night, you should go ahead and get drunk," Noah says.

"You know I do not drink," I say.

"Yeah, that is right. Mr. Straight, how could I forget?" Noah says, laughing.

I have never enjoyed drinking or wanted to drink. I got enough of alcohol watching my father drink himself to death. I look across and see her, Daniela Morris. I cannot help but watch her walk into the reception. At least on this night of hell, I can see her beautiful face.

"Well, is that flame still burning?" Noah says.

I have always had a crush on Daniela, but we come from separate sides of town. Her family is wealthy, and mine, well, we are just your typical middle-class working people. I have not seen her since we graduated from high school three years ago. Yet, she is still as beautiful as ever. She went to college, and I became a cop, just like my father.

"Shut up!" I say to Noah. "You should go talk to her. My sister invited her to the wedding, and I know there is not a plus one for a fact. She is single," Noah says.

"She would never talk to me," I say.

"Why not? You are a catch!" Noah says, laughing.

I sit watching her walk across the room in her long pale pink dress, her blonde hair flowing beautifully. She is the most beautiful creature I have ever seen. But, Daniela is not just beautiful; she is kind and has a smile that lights up any room.

Noah jumps up from the bar. "I will be back, my friend," he says as he dashes away. Noah goes straight to Daniela. I see him talking to her and pointing at me. I am going to kill him when this night is over. I want to crawl under something.

Noah returns without Daniela. He smiles like a jackass, and I want to punch him in the face. "Guess what she said, Mr. Perfect," Noah says.

"Why did you do that?" I ask him.

I feel a small hand on my shoulder. I turn around, and Daniela is standing behind me. "Hi," I say. It is all I can manage to get out.

"Hi," she says softly. "I am sorry. My idiot friend here is drunk. I hope he was not rude," I say to her.

"No, he told me that you wanted to dance with me," she says. "He did. I am sorry, Daniela, but I do not dance," I say.

"Ellie, no one calls me Daniela anymore. Just Ellie," she says. "Ellie, I am a terrible dance partner," I say to her. "I am a great teacher, come on," she says. She reaches for my hand. How can I say no to her?

I take her hand, and she leads me to the dance floor. A slow song is playing as she gets close to me. "I promise I do not bite, John," she says. "I am sorry, I am a little nervous," I say. I smile at her. I feel like an idiot standing here, letting her lead me.

"See, you are not so bad; you are doing great," she says. "What did Noah say to you?" I ask Ellie. "He said that you were dying to ask me for my number but that you were scared of me. Are you scared of me, John?" she asks me.

"No, I am not scared of you. I did not think you would ever give me your number or talk to me," I say.

"Hmmm. So you are afraid of me," Ellie says, laughing. That smile. "Okay, fine, I am terrified of you," I say.

"I tell you what, John. I will give you my phone number on one condition," Ellie says.

"What is that?" I ask her. "You have to promise me that you will call me tonight after you drop me off at home," Ellie says.

"Oh, you need a ride home?" I ask her.

"Yes, I came with my mother, and I would be forever grateful if you got me out of here," Ellie says.

"Deal, I do not want to be here either," I say.

"Really, you do not want to be here with me?" Ellie asks.

"No, No, No. I want to be here with you, just not at this wedding reception. Noah dragged me here," I say.

"So, are we ditching this wedding reception or what?" Ellie asks.

"Let's do it," I say to her.

Ellie leads me off of the dance floor, and we sneak out the back. We run across the parking lot for my car like two kids playing hide and seek. We jump into my truck laughing.

Present DAY

"John, John, John," Ellie says my name over and over in her sleep. I rub her hand, waiting for the nurse to come back with her release papers.

The door opens, and the nurse finally comes into the room. "Dr. Newbern has her orders ready. I called an ambulance to take her home. They will be up in a few minutes if you want to go ahead home and wait for her. Home health should meet you there," the nurse says.

"Thank you," I say to the nurse.

I kiss Ellie on the forehead. "I will see you at home, my love," I say to her. I leave the room. I cannot help but break down as I walk to the elevator. I am not ready to lose her. I know it is coming, but I am not prepared.

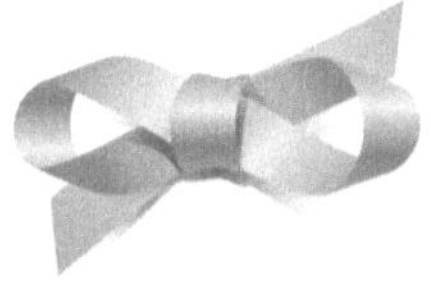

Chapter Three

✳ *Flashback**

    Ellie POV

I slip into a pale pink dress and pink sandals. I look for my pink designer purse. I cannot keep up with anything anymore. I go downstairs to see if I left it in the living room. I hear the car already outside to take me to the wedding reception. I missed the wedding, but I will make the reception. My mother will kill me if I do not make an appearance at her best friend Teresa's daughter's wedding. Maybe it will not be too bad. I might see some people from high school.

I left for college right after graduation, but I had to return due to severe migraines and fatigue. I will start back next semester. In the meantime, I plan to work for my father and rest as much as possible. I finally locate my purse and run out the door to a very annoyed driver.

"Your mother is going to kill me if I do not get you to the reception?" the driver says.

"Relax, William, it is only fifteen minutes away," I say as I get into the car. I miss driving. The doctor says I cannot drive until the migraines stop.

William gets into the car. "You do realize you are very late, miss," William says.

"I am sorry. You are waiting for me, right?" I ask him.

"No, I believe your mother will be bringing you home," William says.

"Damn, I will find a friend to bring me home. I cannot deal with her trying to nurse me today. I am just fine," I say.

William looks at me and grins. I am fine. I am only tired. I wish everyone would give me some space. William drives the fifteen minutes to the reception hall. I get out of the car before he can open the door for me. I am not in the mood to be here. I just want to get this over with as quickly as possible.

I walk into the reception. I look around, looking for the bride and groom. Everyone seems to be having a wonderful time. The room is decorated mainly blue, with fairy lights everywhere. It is so dark in here. At least I do not have to worry about getting a headache. I look over to see Noah making a mad dash for me.

"Hey, Daniela," Noah slurs. He has obviously had a lot to drink. "Celebrating your sister's wedding, I see," I say.

"It is really good to see you," Noah slurs. "You too," I say. I start to make my way in the other direction when he takes my arm. "Listen, John is here, and he wants you to come to talk to him," Noah says.

"Oh, he does. Where is he?" I ask. Noah points to the bar. John Bradley, wow, I always thought he was hot. He was on the football team, and I was a cheerleader, but he never talked to me. I believe he ran in the other direction any time I got near him.

"He is over at the bar," Noah says, pointing at John. I look over and see him. Wow, I look over to see John sitting at the bar. He looks like he wants to be here as much as I do.

"I have to find mother and your sister, and then I will be over to say hi," I say. "Cool," Noah says as he walks away. I watch him walk back to the bar. I make my rounds quickly to let my mother know I made it, and I speak to the beautiful bride. If I had driven myself, I could duck out of here now, but now I am stuck here. At least John can keep me company if he does not run away when he sees me.

I walk over to the bar. I tap him on the shoulder. He turns around and smiles at me when he sees me. I smile back. His beautiful eyes and smile make me melt. I have always had a crush on him.

"Hi," I say to him. John makes a quick apology for Noah getting me over to him. He has no idea how happy it made me that he wanted to say hi. Men are intimidated by me because of my family. It is hard to meet someone. They hear my last night and then run. I am not my family.

I spend the next thirty minutes wrapped in his arms on the dance floor. When John held me and clumsily danced with me, I felt something I have never felt before in my life. Strange that one interaction made me feel so much in such a short amount of time.

I convince John to ditch the wedding. We sneak out the back door and run across the parking lot to his truck.

"Will your mother not be looking for you?" John says.

I laugh. "It will be fine," I say. He opens the door, and I get into his truck. "Where do you want to go?" John asks me. "Anywhere with you," I answer him.

We drive twenty minutes to the lake. He pulls into the parking lot, and we walk down to the water. The lake has a lovely sandy area that my father had put in when he was mayor. The parking lot was his idea too. I think it messed up the look of the lake, but what do I know.

We sit down in the sand close to the water. "I have a blanket in the truck if you don't want to mess up your dress," John says.

"I hate this dress," I answer him. "You shouldn't. You are breathtaking in it," John says.

"Thanks," I say.

We talk for hours about his work as a police officer, his family, and his messy breakup. I talk about school and how I want to go back. It is nice to have someone listen and not try to tell me what I need to do with my life.

"I guess you should drive me home, John," I say. John leans over and kisses me softly. "Sorry, I have wanted to do that since high school, and just in case I never got a chance to do it again," John says. I lean in and kiss him. "I wasn't going to miss the opportunity in case you never call me," I say, smiling at him.

John walks me back to the truck, holding my hand. "Are you going to call me?" I ask him.

"Hell yes!" John answers.

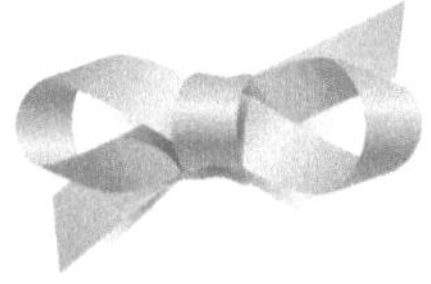

Chapter Four

John POV

I drop Ellie off at her house and drive home to my farmhouse. After my father died, my mother moved into an apartment and let me have the farmhouse. It is small, but I love the land and being on the farm. My sister Crissy never cared about the farm when we were growing up, but I loved it here. I could see myself growing old here with someone and raising a family. Mother wanted to put all the bad memories behind her and make new ones somewhere else, but there was no way she would sell the place. She knew how much it meant to me.

I park my truck and go inside. I want out of this suit and to relax. I have to work the early shift tomorrow. I will call Ellie after work. I cannot believe how the night went tonight. It started out terrible and ended with a kiss from the most beautiful creature on earth. I can still smell the sweet scent of her perfume lingering in the air around me.

I lay out my uniform for in the morning. I know I will be hustling to get out the door at six a.m., and it is already late. I need sleep; as I lay down in my bed, the phone rings. I get up to get the phone in the kitchen. I need to put a phone in my bedroom. Who in the hell could be calling me at this hour? I hope it is not work.

I pick up the phone, and before I can even say hello, I hear the sweetest voice on the other end of the line. "John," Ellie says. "Yes," I respond.

"I hope you are still awake," Ellie says.

"I am awake," I say.

"Good, I wanted to ask you something," Ellie says.

"I see, go ahead," I say. I am curious.

"I was wondering if, and I know this is very forward of me, but I was wondering if you might want to see me tomorrow," Ellie asks me.

"I have to work until six, but I would love to see you. Do you want me to pick you up?" I ask her.

"That would be great. I will see you after six," Ellie says.

"I will come straight after work," I say.

"Okay, see you tomorrow, John," Ellie says and hangs up the phone.

I hang up the phone in the kitchen. I go to bed. I have to get some sleep before I work twelve hours tomorrow. I do not know if I can sleep now, knowing I will get to see her tomorrow. How did this happen? It is crazy.

My alarm is beeping and annoying at five. I get up out of bed. I take a quick shower and get into my uniform. I grab a cup of coffee and stand on the porch waiting for Jeff to pull up to pick me up. Jeff and I have worked together for the last year. He is a good guy and a damn good cop. He knew my father well. After my father died, he took me under his wing and helped me adapt to life as a cop. He is my mentor and father figure.

Jeff pulls into the drive. I walk out to the police car and get into it. "Why in the hell are you so perky this morning?" Jeff asks me as soon as I get into the car.

"I did not realize I was perky," I say, laughing.

"Well, you are, and it is annoying already," Jeff says.

"I met someone, well. I already knew her, so I saw someone last night I have not seen in a long time," I say.

"Oh, yeah, well, I do not want any details," Jeff says. He is always a straight shooter.

"I was not planning on giving any to you. Besides, there is nothing to tell; we are going out tonight," I say.

"I do not want any tomorrow either, and try not to be so perky in the morning. It is too early for that shit," Jeff says.

"I will try," I say.

Jeff drives us to the police station. We have a roll call and get our orders for the day. Jeff and I are usually in the same part of town, doing the same thing every day. Our town is quiet, and everyone knows everyone. So it did not take long for everyone to know that I was with the one that snuck off with Ellie last night.

At the end of the shift, Jeff drives me home. "Listen, young buck; I am just an old man who does not know shit, but be careful with that family. You know, do not piss them off. You don't want to have a career change over a girl," Jeff says to me when I get out of the police car.

"It is just a date, but I understand what you are saying, and I will be careful," I say.

I go into the house to change. As I unlock the door, my phone is ringing. I rush to the phone and answer it. "Hello," I say into the phone.

"John, it is Ellie," she says.

"I am about to change clothes, and I will be on my way," I say.

"Is it okay if I have a driver bring me?" Ellie says.

"That will be fine. I do not mind picking you up," I say.

"I am on my way, and I am bringing dinner," Ellie says.

"See you soon," I say.

My house is a mess. I take a quick shower and change. I begin trying to clean the house before she arrives, but as I am hustling to clean the house, she walks into the door carrying take-out. She sets the food bags down on the coffee table and hugs me.

"I can help you clean the house, but first, let's eat. I know you have had a long day," Ellie says.

I cannot remember the last time someone offered to help me or feed me or even give a damn about what kind of day I had.

"I am sorry this place is a mess," I say.

Ellie sits down on the couch and begins taking the white boxes out of the food bags. "Sit, John, you need to eat," Ellie says.

She hands me a take-out box and a plastic fork. She smiles at me. Damn, I cannot be falling in love with her this fast. It is crazy. She is going to rip my heart out and hand it to me.

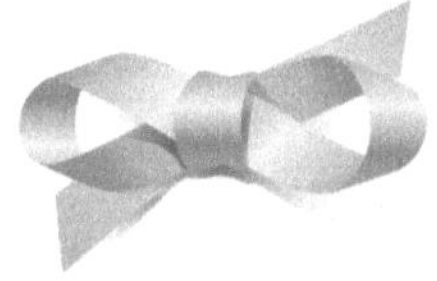

Chapter Five

P resent Day
John POV

I pull into the farmhouse to get ready for Ellie's arrival. My mother, Missy, is waiting for me when I pull up. She comes out to the truck to greet me. I knew she would be here for Ellie.

"Hello, son, I thought you could use some help," my mother says. Mother is getting older, but she has a lot of grit, and she loves Ellie. Honestly, I cannot think of a person that does not love Ellie.

"Home health is on its way with the things she will need. I do not know what you could do, but I am happy you are here mom," I say to her.

I get out of the truck. She hugs me so tightly. I begin to cry. I feel weak. I want to scream. The thought of living my life without Ellie is too much for me. "Let it out, son. You don't want to be a mess in front of Ellie. We have to be strong for her," Mother says.

"I know," I say to her. My tiny mother holds me as I let out every ounce of pain I have held onto through this ordeal. The things Ellie and I have been through would bring an average couple to their knees. We have lost so much in our marriage, but one thing is always true we have loved one another.

Mother and I walk into the house. She has already started cleaning. I can smell pine in the air when I go into the door. Ellie always kept our home spotless. I, on the other hand, am a terrible housekeeper. Over the last three weeks, while she has been in the hospital, I have let the house go. Between work, the hospital, and trying to keep myself pulled together, I have not been able to bring myself to do anything. Thank goodness for mom.

"John, son, have you called her parents?" my mother asks, even though she knows the answer.

"No, I guess I should, but I want to wait on Ellie. Mother, you know how she feels about how they have treated her over the years since she married me," I say.

"They need to know what is going on with their daughter. All of the bad needs to be in the past; Ellie needs everyone right now," my mother says.

"I know, but you know I will not go against Ellie, no matter what," I say.

Ellie has not spoken to her parents since Leah died. She has never forgiven them for not coming to the funeral, and I do not think she ever will. The way they acted when we got married was horrible, but to shun Ellie and not support her in the death of their grandchild, she will never forgive them, not even now at the end of her life.

"John, she needs to talk to her parents. Try to encourage her. They deserve to say goodbye to her if they choose to," my mother says.

"Is Crissy coming?" I ask my mother, trying to change the subject. Crissy has always been close with Ellie. My sweet sister loves Ellie like she is her sister. Crissy has been with Ellie and helped her so much over the years.

"I talked to her earlier. She will be here tonight to help you. I thought I would cook something for Ellie, and we could spend time with her," my mother says.

"She does not want us treating her like she is dying, and you know that just be here for her but don't go too far out of the way. She hates that, mom," I say.

"I love Ellie. I am going to stay here with you until the end. I will try not to dote on her too much, but you know how much I love her and want her to be comfortable. I do not want her to have to worry about anything," my mother says.

"Thank you," I say.

"I set myself up in the guest room. I will stay out of the way," my mother says.

"No, you won't," I say. The thought of my mother staying out of the way is laughable. She loves Ellie like a daughter. Since Ellie has been sick, she has endured my mother cooking, cleaning, shopping for her, and doing anything she thought was helpful. Ellie lets her and never fusses. Even when my mother rearranged the living room to make it more comfortable for Ellie, Ellie did not like it, but she thanked her and let it go. They are both headstrong, and damn they are just alike. Maybe that is why they get along so well. They are exactly alike.

"Home health is here with Ellie's supplies. Do you want me to handle it?" my mother asks.

"Please, I need a shower before Ellie gets here," I say to my mother.

"Go ahead, son. I will take care of everything," my mother says, motioning for me to go ahead. I know she is worried about me. There is no need. I will be fine for now. In the day to come, not so much but for now, I am surviving.

I go into the bathroom and turn on the water. I need one more breakdown before Ellie gets here. I have so many decisions to make for her. She hates not being in complete control of her life. Who would have thought a love like ours would end up here.

I hear the hustle and bustle in the house as I try to shower and have a private moment to myself. There will not be many of these from now on, just an endless parade of people and nurses for Ellie. I need time with her, just us. I do not know how I will make that happen, but I will figure it out. I have so much I want to say to her before I lose her. I want her to know how she saved me from myself. I want her to know how much I love her before this is over.

Chapter Six

Ellie POV

The smell of the hospital and all the noise is getting to me. I want to go home and be with my husband and my animals. I have so much I want to do with the time I have left. I am so sleepy. I close my eyes and hear someone come into my room. I open my eyes to see Patsy standing at my bedside.

"I was going just to leave when I saw you were sleeping," Patsy says.

"It is fine. I am happy to see you," I say. I try to push myself up in the bed, but it isn't easy. Patsy tries to help me. "It is fine, Patsy," I say to her. I look at her sweet face. She smiles at me. What a glimmer of light she is in this horrible place.

"Joshua told me you were leaving, and I wanted to come by and see you," Patsy says.

Patsy and I have been friends since high school. We were both cheerleaders. Patsy married Joshua, my doctor. Every time I have been here, she has been to see me and convinced me to stay a few times longer than I wanted to stay.

"I hope Joshua did not recruit you to convince me to stay here?" I ask.

"No, he knows I will always take your side. I only wanted to see my friend," Patsy says.

"I am not dead yet, Patsy. You can come to the house when I go home," I say to her.

Patsy begins to laugh and then cry. "Please do not do that," I say to her.

"I am sorry. I wanted to come by for another reason, too, and I did not want to do it at the house because I know how upset John gets about you know your family," Patsy says.

"John does not get upset. He just backs me up; that is all," I say.

"Your brother wants to see you. So he asked me to come to you and see if you will see him," Patsy says.

"No, not right now, but I will think about it, okay," I say to her.

"Thomas does not know what is going on, and I would never say anything to him, but you should see him," Patsy says.

"I will think about it, but since you are here, there is something you can help me with, if you don't mind," I say.

"Sure, anything," Patsy says.

"Tell Joshua I said thank you," I say.

"For what?" Patsy asks.

"He knows," I answer.

Flashback

"Daniela, there is a young man here to see you, Joshua. He is such a sweet boy. You know his entire family is doctors, and he is in medical school," my mother says to me as I walk down the staircase to the front door.

I greet Joshua at the door. "We are going to the lake and dinner," I say as I exit the door with Joshua quickly.

We walk out the door to his sports car. Joshua opens the door, and I get into the car. I look back to see my mother and father watching me leave with the doctor's son. I am sure they are so proud.

"You know, for a grown woman to be sneaking around is a little weird, don't you think?" Joshua says.

"I know, but I have to do this for a little while. I do not want to cause any trouble for John, and you know how my father is about John's family," I say.

"You owe me big," Joshua says as he drives me to John's house.

"I will dance at your wedding," I say, laughing.

"I would have to meet someone first," Joshua says.

"You will, Josh. You are a great man and a damn good friend. Any woman would be lucky to have you," I say to him.

"Yeah, you think so," Joshua says.

"Yes, doc, I do," I say.

"I am not a doctor yet," Joshua says.

"Hurry up; I need someone to figure out why I am having headaches," I say to him.

Joshua pulls into John's farmhouse. John comes out to meet us. "Thanks, Josh," John says.

"You kids don't get into any trouble. I will be back after my study group," Joshua says.

John takes me into his arms as Joshua drives away. He leans in and kisses me. "I hate all this sneaking around," John says.

"Think of it as an adventure," I say to him.

Present Day

"Ellie Ellie Ellie," I hear my voice, but I cannot open my eyes. "I think she is having a seizure; get Dr. Newbern," Patsy screams.

"Ellie, come back to us," I hear her voice saying. It echoes loudly in my ears.

"Ellie, please, Ellie," Patsy pleads.

I feel cold and damp. "Ellie," I hear Dr. Newbern say my name.

"Joshua, I need to get to John. Can you drive me? Please don't tell my parents," I whisper to him.

I feel cold again, and then I open my eyes to a beeping noise and Joshua. "Ellie, look at me," Joshua says.

"Hi Joshua," I say softly.

"I disapprove of you leaving here. Please stay another week," Joshua says to me.

I begin to cry. "I have to go home to John. I need to be at the beginning when it ends," I say.

"Ellie, I can give you more time with him. Is it your dogs? I will march them in here myself to see you, please, listen to me, as your doctor and your friend," Joshua pleads with me.

I reach out, and I touch Joshua's face. "I do not have a lot of time left; please let me go home," I say. I look over to Patsy. Her face is red from crying. I reach out and touch Joshua's hand. "Please do not tell John about this. I have not had this kind of episode in a while, please," I plead with him.

Joshua shakes his head and agrees not to say anything. "You are on a lot of pain medicine. Unfortunately, this will happen again," Joshua says. Patsy leaves the room crying as the EMT's come into the room to take me home.

Chapter Seven

John POV

"John, you have a phone call, it is important, or I would not bother you," my mother says through the door. I step out of the shower and wrap up in a towel. I crack the door open, and she hands me my cell phone in through the tiny opening. I cannot believe I left my phone. What the hell was I thinking? What if Ellie needed me.

"Hello," I say.

"John, It is Patsy. I just went to see Ellie," Patsy says, her voice breaking.

"What is wrong? Is she okay?" I ask frantically.

"Yes, she is on her way home to you now, but I wanted to tell you something because she made Joshua promise not to say a word," Patsy says.

"What is it?" I ask.

My mind is racing a thousand places. What the hell would prompt Patsy to go against Ellie and her husband?

"She had a seizure at the hospital right before they left with her. Joshua said it was from all the pain medicines she is on to control the pain. I only wanted you to prepare yourself because it will happen again," Patsy says.

"Thank you," I say. I hang up the phone and set it down on the sink. I grab the sink and hold it hard in my hands. I want to rip it out of the wall and throw it. I want to scream and cry. I kneel down on the floor and sob. My mother comes back to the door.

"Is she okay, John! Is Ellie okay?" my mother screams. I wipe my face with my towel and get out of the floor. I open the door. I look at my mother and grab her. "She is okay. That was Patsy. She said Ellie had a seizure from the pain medicines, but she did not want me to know," I say.

"She is still trying to protect you," my mother says. She holds me tightly. "I need to dress before she gets here. Patsy said the ambulance is on its way with her," I say.

"Home health is set up. I had her bed put in the sunroom. She loves that room," my mother says.

"She will love that, mom," I say.

"Do you want me to stay until she gets here, or can I run to the store?" my mother asks.

"We have plenty of everything here. What do you need?" I ask.

My mother puts her hands on her hips and gives me one hell of a look. "John Bradley, this house needs food. Ellie needs good food, and I will go get it for her," my mother says.

"Hang on a moment and let me get dressed. Then, I will give you some money," I say to her.

"John, you can text me if you think of anything she needs. I will be right back," my mother says as she leaves.

"Do you know how to text?" I ask her. "Funny, glad you still have your sense of humor," my mother says as she exits my bedroom. I dress quickly and go to the sunroom to wait for Ellie.

I sit in the sunroom next to Ellie's bed. One of her dogs has already claimed a spot next to her bed. I guess he knows this is where Ellie will be sleeping. My mother put her favorite blanket on the hospital bed and a cot next to it for me to sleep on to be close to her.

Ellie and I never spent many nights apart except for extended hospital stays and when she lost herself for a bit after Leah died. My sweet Ellie, there are so many moments with you that I have to cherish.

Flash Back

"Stay away from my daughter!" A tall, well-dressed man coming running into the police station screaming and coming straight for me, Mark Morris, I can only presume.

I do not acknowledge him at first. I want him to come to me before I respond to him. I promised Ellie I would not get into a confrontation with him, but he is coming into my work and starting with me.

"Did you hear me? You cannot take care of my Daniela," Mark screams at me.

"I heard you. I choose not to respond," I say and turn to walk away.

Mark grabs me, which is a huge mistake. We are in a small police station with many witnesses, but Mark is someone who has a lot of pull. If I knock his ass out, I will be the one in trouble.

"Do you want to do this here, Mr. Morris?" I ask him.

"I want you to stay away from her. When I am done with you, you will be scrubbing toilets," he continues to scream.

Lucky for me the chief likes me, or Mr. Mark Morris might be able to have pulled it off. "Mark, even if I am scrubbing toilets, I will still love her and be with her. So do what you want," I say to him.

I walk away from him. It was the hardest thing to do. I wanted to put him in the ground, but Ellie, she makes me a better person. So I walked away from the meanest bastard in town, Ellie's father.

I walk out of the police station and get into the car with Jeff. "I need to find a phone and call Elli," I say.

"Do you love that girl?" Jeff asks me.

I look at him. Jeff never really asks me anything. He loves to give out advice, but he doesn't ask for input before ripping me a new asshole.

"I do love her more than anything in this world," I answer him.

"Well, that is obvious. I cannot believe you did not plant him where he was standing. But that is not the point, young buck. What you need to do is go buy a ring and marry that girl now!" Jeff says.

"You think so," I say.

"Yeah, I do. But I am done talking about it now. Just do it, and I do not want any details," Jeff says. I think I saw him smile when he told me to marry her.

Chapter Eight

Ellie POV
The ambulance ride is long. I feel like the EMTs are looking at me like I am crazy for wanting to go home. Everyone thinks I am crazy. I need to go home; it is the only place I want to be right now. I want to be with John every night and his family. They are the only ones that have ever really cared about me and how I feel. I need to be with them.

Flash Back

I have tried to call John several times, but he has not answered his phone. I know he has to be home by now. It is almost eight. That is it; I am going over there. I run down the stairs. I will just drive even though I am not supposed to drive right now. I do not have a headache right now; I think I can make it.

I run into my father at the bottom of the steps. I do not want to talk to him after what he did today. "Where are you off to in such a rush?" my father asks.

"Out, I am going out," I answer.

"Are you driving?" my father asks.

"I do not have a choice unless you will give me a driver," I answer him.

"There is no one to drive you to that man," my father snaps at me.

"I know what you did today. What is wrong with you?" I scream at him.

"If you leave here tonight, I am done with you, Daniela," my father says, thinking it will stop me from leaving.

"Fine," I say to him.

I run back up the stairs and pack a bag quickly. Then, I come running down the stairs past my father. "Where are you going?" he asks me.

"You said you do not want me here, so bye, father," I say as I go out the door.

I go to my car parked in the driveway. I will drive slowly. It is not far. If I need to stop, I will. I can do this. I paid for this car he cannot stop me from taking it. I get into the car and start it. My father comes out of the house, my mother behind him. They are both screaming. I cannot handle this anymore. I just need to go. I am not sure where I will go, but I will figure it out after talking to John.

I pull out of the driveway and begin my drive to John's farmhouse. I drive very slowly. I make it almost to John's house when I am pulled over. I stop the car on the side of the road and wait for the police officer to come up to the window.

"Ma'am, why are you driving so slowly? Are you okay?" the officer asks me.

I begin to cry when I see it is John. "I was trying to get to you," I say.

"Move over, and I will drive you the rest of the way, hang on a minute and let me tell Jeff," John says.

I move over to the passenger seat. John returns to the car quickly and takes over the drive.

"Where have you been?" I ask him.

"I had an errand to run after work, and Jeff helped me with it; when we saw your car, I told him to pull you over," John says.

"I had a fight with my father," I say, crying.

"Funny, I fought with him today too. He must be making his rounds today," John says.

"I know; I am so sorry he did that to you. I was afraid you would stop seeing me because of him," I say to John.

"No, never. I love you, Ellie," John says.

"You do; you love me," I say. He has never said that he loved me before tonight.

"Yes, more than anything. You are my world, Ellie," John says.

We pull into John's farmhouse. He grabs my bag out of the car and opens my door. He takes my hand, and we walk into his house. His house is a mess as usual.

"Ellie, I have something very important I need to talk about with you," John says.

"Okay," I say. I sit down on the couch. John sets my bag down. He takes a small box out of his pocket and opens it.

"It is not much. I would love to give you the biggest diamond in the world. This ring was my mothers' wedding ring. Jeff drove me to get it after work. I want you to be my wife. I realize we have not been dating long, but you would make me so happy. I would do everything to make you happy," John says. He stumbles over his words. He is so nervous.

I sit silently for a second, and then I smile at him. "I have one condition," I say to him.

"What is that?" he asks.

"No matter what, we always work it out; we are in this forever," I say to him.

"I can live with that," John says.

I kiss John and smile at him. "Yes, John Bradley, I will be your wife," I say to him.

John pulls me close to him and holds me so tightly. "I hate to ruin this moment, but I promised my mother I would call her the moment you said yes," John says, laughing.

"Do you want me to call her?" I ask John. "Come on, we can do it together," John says. "Oh, one more thing, my father kicked me out of the house; I need a place to stay," I say to John.

"Well, I have extra rooms, take one. I will not have you in my bed until we are married," John says.

"Such a gentlemen," I say to him.

John picks up the phone to call his mother. He hands me the phone so that I can tell her first. He is beaming. At this moment, I am so happy, and then my head begins to hurt. I drop the receiver as the phone rings and fall to my knees.

"Ellie, are you okay?" John asks.

"I need the red pill in my purse," I say to him. John rushes to my purse and brings me the pill. Then, he gets a glass of water from the kitchen.

"Ellie, how sick are you?" John asks.

"I don't know. The doctors have no idea what is wrong with me. Can you handle all of this?" I ask him.

"I would walk through hell for you, Ellie," John says to me.

The phone rings. John lets it ring. It took forty-five minutes for the medicine to work on my headache. When it finally went away, we call John's mother to tell her the news. She is thrilled and happy for us. My parents will not be, but I do not care.

Chapter Nine

John POV
Flash Back

Ellie's father took her off his insurance the day after she left. She was lucky and got a job in the school system a few days later. She was a nervous wreck which made her headaches worse. There were a lot of horrible nights until she was able to secure a job. Jeff thinks I do not know, but he paid for her medication when he heard about what her father did to her. I do not know how I will ever repay him for what he did. I can add Ellie to my insurance after we are married. I wanted to give her the wedding she dreamed of, but we cannot wait months to get married in reality. We need to get married right away.

"We can just go to the courthouse, John," Ellie says to me.

"I do not want you to think you have to get married in the courthouse. We can have a small wedding here at the farm, just family," I say to her.

"We do not have to be in a rush just because my father is crazy. This is what he wants. He wants me to panic and come running home," Ellie says.

"I know you are marrying me because you love me not to spite your father. We can do it here with our family," I say.

Ellie reaches for me, tears in her eyes. "John, I have no family," Ellie says. She is serious. The moment she chooses me over them, they are done with her.

"You have my family and me. We are all the family you will ever need, I promise you, Ellie. My mother loves you, and Crissy loves you. Hell, I think Jeff even kind of likes you," I say to her.

"Okay, let's plan a small wedding for the farmhouse. Do you think your mother and sister would help me?" Ellie asks.

I shake my head. "Be prepared for both of them to take over the entire event," I say.

Ellie jumps up from the couch. She grabs me and hugs me tightly. "I wish they would just plan it for me. I am not good at planning things," Ellie says.

"Oh, I am sure they will both love that. My sweet Ellie, you have no idea how happy it will make both of them to plan this wedding," I say.

Ellie kisses me softly. I pull her close to me. My breathing becomes labored as I touch her body. We decided to wait until we are married, but it is getting harder not to want more from her. I want to be with her in every way. Ellie's hands slide down the front of my shirt. I can tell she is getting uncomfortable.

"I am sorry," I say.

Ellie leans forward and kisses me again. I kiss her back with more passion this time. We stand in the living room, kissing as her hand finds its way into my hair. She lets her hand wander from my hair to my neck, down my shoulder. She steps back from me and unbuttons her top. She exposes her white lace bra to me. I am in awe of her beauty. There is nothing I want more than to take her right now.

"I want to wait until we are married, but there is no reason why we cannot have a little fun," Ellie says to me.

"I do not want you to do anything you do not want right now. I can wait," I say, looking at her beautiful body as she begins to undress in front of me.

"I guess I can allow you to see the goods before you marry me," Ellie says, laughing.

She is in front of me in her white lace bra and panties. She is so incredible. She takes my hand and leads me to her bedroom. This is probably a good idea because her room is much cleaner than mine will ever be in this lifetime.

"Ellie, you don't have to do this," I say to her as she leads me into her room.

"I want to be with you tonight, John, in every way except one. I do not want us to have sex until we are married, but there are so many things we can do to be together and love one another besides that, okay," Ellie says softly to me.

"Okay," I say to her.

Ellie leads me into her bedroom. She unbuttons my shirt and lets her hands run across my chest. She kisses my lips and then my chest. She is so sensual and sexy. I feel a rise in my pants as she continues to touch me all over. Finally, she removes my shirt and lets it drop to the floor. Her kisses are amazing as she unzips me and removes my pants.

I get into bed with Ellie. I have no idea what this night will hold or what she has planned for us. I kiss her neck and move to her breast, still in her bra. "May I remove this?" I ask her. "Yes," Ellie answers.

I remove her bra and touch her soft skin. I kiss her breast and then begin to suck her nipple. Elli arches her back. "John, I am a virgin," Ellie says to me. Of course, I already knew that, but she needed me to know.

"I don't want to give myself to you, and then you change your mind about marrying me. It would crush me," Ellie says.

"There is nothing that will stop me from marrying you," I say to her.

Ellie pulls me closer to her. I am between her legs, pressed against her. The only thing between us is the thin fabric of our underwear, and I want her so badly. I kiss her neck, and I cannot help but grind myself against her sweet spot. Ellie lets out a soft moan.

"I want you so bad," Ellie says to me.

"I want you too, but I won't. I know how bad you want to wait," I say, breathing heavy. I would love to plunge into her and give her pleasure.

I let my hand wander between her legs. I touch her middle and begin to massage her. Ellie moans as I massage her. I let my fingers slip under the fabric of her panties. I kiss her as I let my fingers dip into her. Ellie bites my bottom lip and moans as I finger her.

"Damn, John, you are making it hard for me to say no," Ellie says. I stop. I kiss her on the lips. "Why did you stop?" Ellie asks me.

"Because I will not have you regretting it when I make love to you," I say. Ellie smiles at me. "You are going to love me forever, aren't you?" Ellie says. "Yes, I am," I tell her.

Ellie pulls me back down onto her. "Make love to me, John," Ellie says softly.

Chapter Ten

Ellie POV

The ambulance pulls into the house with me in tow. I feel like a sideshow that everyone is coming out to get a good look at for a dollar. The driver pulls up close to the house. The two EMTs open the door and begin to take me into the house. I wish they would let me out of this stupid and give me a walker. I can get myself into the house. There is no need for all of these theatrics.

I look over to see my darling mother-in-law, Missy waiting on me. Where is John, I wonder? He is probably trying to piece the house back together. I hope he is resting. He has worked himself to death over the last few weeks. I worry about him.

Missy reaches over and takes my hand as the EMTs wheeled me into the house and this very unstable gurney. I feel like I am going to fall through it. "Take her all the way to the back of the house, in the sunroom," Missy instructs them.

She has moved my bed to the sunroom. Bless her for being here. I love the sunroom. It is the perfect place for me to be. It is warm and beautiful. I can see the yard, the pond, and I can watch my dogs play.

The EMTs take me to the sunroom. John is waiting for me there. I smile at him. He looks tired and worried. Oh, my, sweetheart, I hate I have caused you all of this pain. But, it will be over soon, and then you can rebuild without me.

I am pulled over into the bed by the EMTs. The EMTs exit and speak to Missy on the way out of the house. John tries to make me comfortable in the bed. He knows how much I hate to be fussed over for any reason.

"John, stop; I can fix myself in the bed," I say as he fluffs pillows and moves blankets.

He sighs at me for fussing at him. "I just want you to be comfortable, that is all," John says.

"I am fine. I don't need anything other than maybe a cherry soda," I say. "I will get it for you," he says and rushes away. I take a deep breath and try to fix the bed myself.

"It is okay to ask for help," Missy says, watching as I try to fix myself in the bed. "I am fine, I promise; I do not want you or John or anyone treating me like...." I start to say.

"Like what? That you are sick. Ellie, you are sick, and you need our help. Stop pretending you do not need us because you do," Missy says to me.

I rise up a little. "Can you fix this pillow?" I ask her. Missy comes to my rescue. She fluffs the pillow perfectly. "Don't worry, I will not tell John you let me help you," Missy says. I smile at her. I love her. She is always there for me and has loved me as one of her own since before John and I married.

Flash Back

"Missy, I need your help," I say into the phone.

"What is it, dear?" Missy asks.

"I have to find a dress, and I am so overwhelmed. I cannot seem to get it together. I cannot even find my damn car keys," I say.

I begin to sob into the phone. "We are on our way to pick you up now. Crissy and I will take you shopping," Missy says.

I hang up the phone. Was I supposed to go shopping with them today? I cannot remember. I check my calendar John made me. Yes, I am going to town with them today. My brain is not working today. It is the new medicine that is supposed to help but seems to cause memory loss from time to time.

I sit down on the couch and wait for Missy and Crissy to come to pick me up. What if I forget who I am or who John is? I cannot take this medicine anymore. I will deal with the headaches. I want to cry, but I need to get ready to go to town. I look down, wait I am dressed and ready to go already. I am confused.

Missy comes into the house with Crissy. "Are you okay?" Missy asks me. "No, it is the new meds. I do not want to take the meds anymore. It is supposed to help with my headaches, but it is making me forget things. Also, the wedding is in a few weeks, and I have no idea what has been done or needs to be done," I say.

Missy kneels in front of me. "Ellie, the wedding is tomorrow. We got your dress weeks ago. We are going to get our nails done today," Missy says.

I look at her, confused. "Oh, I don't feel like myself," I say to her. "Why don't I call the doctor and see what he thinks?" Missy suggests. "I think you should," I say to her. Missy goes into the kitchen to call my doctor and explain to him what is going on with me.

Crissy sits down beside me. "Ellie, you are under a lot of stress from the wedding and the new meds. It is no wonder you forget things. Stop and take it in; just relax a little," Crissy says.

"You are right; I am losing my mind. I bet I am making John crazy," I say.

Crissy reaches over and hugs me. "I have never seen my brother happier than with you," Crissy says to me.

Missy comes back into the living room. "I talked to the nurse, and she thinks it is stress from the wedding and adjusting to the new meds, but she is going to talk to your doctor and call us back," Missy says.

I stand up and smile. "I feel better; we should go," I say. Missy and Crissy look at each other oddly. "I have a better idea. I will call Veronica and have her come here to do our nails," Crissy says.

"Ellie, I am worried about you. We should wait for your doctor to call back," Missy says.

I reluctantly agree. She is right. I should wait for the doctor to call back. Crissy goes into the kitchen to call Veronica to come to the house to do our nails. I am getting married tomorrow. I need my brain to work with me and not against me. I want this to be a happy day for us. I cannot be sick on our wedding day. I do not want to forget this day.

Chapter 11

John POV

Ellie goes to sleep almost immediately after my mother helps her get comfortable in the bed. I look at how she sleeps so peacefully. It reminds me of our wedding night when she passed out and slept for hours on the couch in her wedding dress as soon as the guests left. The memory makes me smile. I want more memories with her.

Flash Back Wedding Day

I asked Jeff to be my best man. It seemed fitting, and I think it made him happy. But, I cannot tell; it is not like the man ever smiles. We only invited a small number of friends and family to our wedding. In reality, Ellie would have loved to have a big wedding, but she did not want to be rejected by her family again.

Ellie's medication has been changed again as of yesterday, which has left her frazzled and worried. She was experiencing some memory lapses. The doctor referred her to a specialist. We are hoping for answers soon. Ellie wants a family but is afraid to even think about a family with her health problems.

"Are you going to smile at all today, Jeff?" I ask Jeff as he stands next to me, waiting for my beautiful bride to make her entrance.

"Probably not, but I almost did when I walked your sister down the aisle. Perks of being the best man, I guess," Jeff says.

"Wow, Jeff, you were almost funny," I say to him. He cracks a small smile, but it is progress.

Ellie makes her entrance. She is breathtaking. She walks out of the side garden door out to the field that our friends helped decorate. I hope she does not regret this small humble wedding. I know I won't. I have everything here I could possibly ever want. All I need is her and her love to carry me through my life.

Ellie takes my hand when she finally reaches her destination next to me. I cannot help but shed tears as we recite our wedding vows. I have never been this happy. I am a bucket of mush, and she seems to be enjoying every second of it. When I finally lift her veil and kiss her as my wife, my face is wet from crying. I will never hear the end of this.

Ellie and I step down from the man-made altar Noah and Steve constructed for our special day as husband and wife. She is happy, and so am I; she looks relieved. Finally, the stress of the wedding is behind us, and we can start a new chapter in our life, a life together just her and me.

The reception goes by fast. My sister made our wedding cake, and my friend Bobby smoked meat for the meal. My mother and sister cooked sides for the reception meal. Crissy's friends served at the reception. Unfortunately, only one friend of Ellie's came to the wedding, and that was Joshua. Crissy introduced Joshua to Patsy at the wedding, and we lost both of them somewhere over the course of the night.

We decided to spend our wedding night in our home and go to the beach in the morning. She did not want to travel exhausted, and she wants to make sure everything is put back in its place and nice and tidy before we leave. How will I live with a clean freak the rest of my life?

Everyone helped clean up after the reception. It did not take long with everyone's help. Everyone in our life came together to make this day special and tried to take as much stress off Ellie as possible, and it is refreshing to see how many people care for us.

Ellie sits down on the couch in the living room in her colossal wedding dress. It is a funny sight to see. "I can help you out of that, you know," I say to her. "I just want to rest a moment," Ellie says. Before the words completely exit her mouth, her eyes close, and she falls asleep in her wedding dress on the couch. I cannot help but laugh. I let her be. I know she is exhausted.

I let her sleep for at least an hour. I love watching her do anything, even sleep. Finally, I decide to take her to bed to get some rest. I scoop her up awkwardly and carry her to our bedroom. Odd to think that she now is in the same room with me; until now, we have slept in separate bedrooms. Only once did we ever skip on our promise to wait until we got married. I can wait another night to sleep with my wife. I know she needs rest.

I carry Ellie to bed. She wakes and looks at me with a smile. "Are you taking me to bed, husband?" Ellie asks.

"Yes, you need rest," I say.

"I have a lifetime to rest. You can help me out of this monster of a wedding dress and have your way with me," Ellie says, laughing as I set her down beside the bed.

I unzip the back of her dress and try my best to undo all of the buttons carefully. I touch her soft back as I help slide the gown down her body. Her white lace bra and panties underneath look sexy on her small frame. For once, my neat and tidy wife doesn't panic to hang something up. Instead, she steps out of the wedding gown, leaving it on the floor, and presses her beautiful body next to mine.

Ellie kisses my lips as she loosens my tie. Her hand moves down to the buttons on my shirt. She works fast, sliding my shirt off of me and letting it hit the floor. I touch her waist and pull her close to me. The heat between Ellie and me is unreal. My hands begin to fondle her breast as I nervously remove her bra. Why am I so nervous? I let my hand move lower, removing her panties and then sliding my hand between her legs. The warmth and wetness of her sweet spot is soaking my fingertips as I thrust my fingers into her. I am quivering like a man who has never had a woman in his bed.

Ellie lets her hands wander down to unzip me and remove my pants. She is ready for me to take her, and honestly, I am eager to be inside her. I want to make love to my wife. We make our way into the bed, kissing and caressing each other as the moment of passion is coming that we have wanted so badly. She stretches her neck as I push into her and begin to thrust into her juiciness. I kiss her neck as I take her. It is maddening to be inside her. Ellie trembles and moans as I thrust deeper into her. I swirl my manhood in her and thrust deeper. Ellie pulls me down to her to kiss her again. Our tongues are gliding over one another as our bodies pressed together, creating the pleasure we both desire.

The thrilling sensation as I swell inside her wanting to release my seed into her, is maddening. I am trying to wait, but being inside this beautiful creature pushes me to want to release myself. I push harder into Ellie, and her body begins to quiver as she releases her orgasm. I kiss her delicate neck as I can no longer hold out and need to release. I push into her again, kissing her neck as I spill my seed into her beautiful body.

I kiss her softly on the lips and then take my place lying behind her. I hold her. She takes my hand in her hand, smiling. "I love you, John," Ellie says. "You have no idea how much I love you, Ellie," I tell her. "Yes, I do," She says. We fall asleep, resting satisfied until morning.

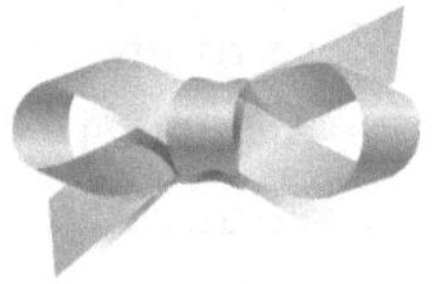

Chapter 12

John POV

Present Day

I awake in the morning. Ellie is resting and does not seem to be in any pain. I watch her sleep for a while. The sun begins to shine into the sunroom, but Ellie continues to rest. I have been watching her sleep for a time, and I need to make her some breakfast. I kiss her on the forehead.

"Rest, my love," I whisper to her. Ellie does not move; she continues to rest peacefully.

I go into the kitchen. My mother and Crissy are already in the kitchen cooking breakfast. Thankfully they made coffee. They both look like they have something on their minds.

"Spill it, you two," I say to them. I know them well enough to know when they have something to say that I am not going to like.

"John, there is something we need to discuss," Crissy says. I can tell she is dreading the conversation. So I am sure it is about Ellie's family.

I sit down at the table to wait for the spill she is about to give me. I know it is hard for her to understand why Ellie does not want to see them. We are a close-knit family. I cannot imagine not speaking to my mother or sister, but Ellie's family is different. They are not like us.

"Thomas wants to see Ellie. He called last night. Someone told him she was sick and that she will probably not be with us much longer," Crissy says.

My mother does not say anything. She has been through this conversation with me many times since Ellie's condition got worse. She knows I will not go against Ellie.

"Crissy, if you want Thomas to see Ellie, then you march your ass into that sunroom, and you tell her that on her death bed, she needs to such it up and see him because I will not do it. I will not force her to see the family that abandoned her. You know the family that cut off her access to medication and doctors when she was sick to try to force her back home. The same family that refused even to show up when Leah died. Go tell her how you feel," I say to Crissy.

My mother sits silently at the table. "I just do not want there to be any regrets for anyone, John, that is all," Crissy says.

"Ellie will not have any regrets. She will be dead—no regrets for her. I will not have any because I will not force a dying woman to spend a moment with people who do not give a shit about her," I say to Crissy.

I have had enough. It is too early in the morning, and I need to focus on Ellie. I grab a biscuit from the stove and fill a coffee cup. I stomp through the house to the front porch. I open the screen door and let it slam as I go out the door. I should not have done that. I hope I did not wake up Ellie.

My mother follows me to the porch. She sits down in a rocking chair beside me on the porch. "You know, John, this is hard for Crissy to understand. If she were sick, she would want you with her," my mother says. "I know that, but she has not been here the last few years. She was not here when I held Ellie after Leah died. Ellie cried for her mother, and she refused to see her. How can a mother do that? Now they want to see her. To hell with them," I say to my mother with tears streaming down my face.

"John, you are the best thing that ever happened to Ellie, and she is the best thing that ever happened to you. Leah was a beautiful baby, and I know how hard that would be on a marriage. But you and Ellie were so strong for each other. I have never seen such a beautiful love between two people," my mother says.

"I do not know how I will live without her in my life. I do not think I can, mom," I say to her.

"Yes, you will live, and you will survive. I will make sure of that, John, my boy. I promised Ellie that I would make sure you would be okay, and you will not make me a liar," my mother says.

"Tell Crissy not to bring this up again, please," I say to my mother. "I will take care of it," my mother says.

I pull myself together to go into the house and feed Ellie breakfast. Ellie's dogs come up on the porch and begin to howl. They miss her. I know I need to let them see her. So I have made them stay in the front of the house until Ellie is awake enough to spend time with them. I pet Skippy on the head, and he turns to the road and starts growling. I look at mom.

"Are we expecting visitors?" I ask my mother.

"No, John. The doctor said to limit visitors for now," my mother says.

I open the door and let the dogs into the house. Crissy comes out on the porch to see why the dogs are growling. "Who is coming up the drive?" Crissy asks.

As we stand there waiting to see who is coming up the drive, Ellie begins to scream. The three of us run into the house to see about Ellie. My heart races as I try to get to Ellie. Her screams ring in my ears. I begin to cry as her screams rip my heart out of my chest.

"Ellie, I am here," I say as I take her hand.

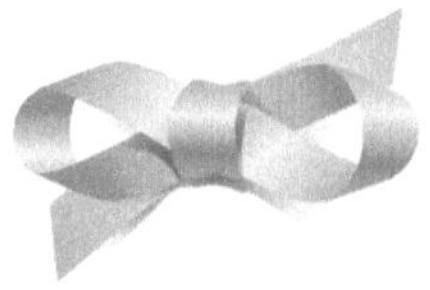

Chapter 13

"Are you feeling okay?" John asks me, concerned.

I pour him coffee into his thermos and hand it to him. I kiss him on the cheek. "I think I have some sort of bug or something. I am going to ask your mother or Crissy to drive me to the doctor," I say.

"I can stay home today if you need me to. I have not used any sick days in case you need me to take off work," John says.

He has not missed any work. On the contrary, he has gone to work sick, tired, and half-dead if he needs to miss because of me. I hate that he does not take care of himself.

"I am fine. I think it is just a bug. If it is anything serious, I will call you, okay," I assure him.

"Do not drive yourself. Promise me you will not drive. My mother or Crissy are happy to help out," John says.

"I know, but I feel like a burden to them," I say.

John pulls me in close to him. I always feel so much comfort in his embrace. "You are not a burden to anyone, not ever. Besides, my mother loves having someone to make a fuss over," John says.

Jeff pulls up to pick up John. I walk John out on the front porch and watch him get into the car with Jeff. Then, I let the dogs into the house to eat. I will call Crissy after I feed the dogs.

I feed the dogs and sit down to eat breakfast. Everything tastes strange. It is probably this new medicine I am taking. It does help the headaches, but unfortunately, everything tastes like garbage. The smell of the kitchen and the taste of my coffee begin to make me feel nauseous. I do not want to spend another morning sick.

I pick up the phone and dial Crissy. "Hello," Crissy says. "Hey Crissy, I know you get sick of me, but I need to go to the doctor today. I am not feeling well," I say. "Sure, sis, I am not busy at all today. We can grab some lunch after we go. First, I need to shower and get dressed," Crissy says. "Okay, I am calling Joshua now to get an appointment," I say. "See you soon; love you," Crissy says as she hangs up the phone.

I have no idea what I would do without John's family. I call Joshua's office, and the nurse tells me just to come as soon as I can. I think they are used to me calling in a panic whenever something goes wrong. I was thrilled when Josh opened up his practice here. He is more than helpful and patient with me.

I am still getting dressed whenever Crissy arrives to take me to the doctor. She comes into the house looking for me. They panic if I do not come straight out, which is ridiculous since I have only passed out once since John and I have been married.

"Ellie, where are you?" Crissy calls to me.

"I am coming, sorry, I have been sick all morning," I say to her.

"I let the dogs out of the house; I hope that is okay?" Crissy asks.

"Yeah, Tim is here to do some work. I am sure they want to supervise him while I am gone," I say.

"What time we need to be there?" Crissy asks.

"The nurse said just to come on when I am ready," I say.

"You look pretty," Crissy says.

It is a lie, but I will take it. My hair started doing something crazy with the new medicine, but John and everybody else pretends not to notice.

"I am thinking about cutting my hair today. What do you think?" I ask her as we walk out of the house.

"I think you would be pretty no matter what you do to your hair," Crissy says.

We get into the car and make the drive to Joshua's office. I have Crissy stop twice so I can be sick. "Do you need me to call John? Are you sure you are okay?" Crissy asks.

"Yes, I am fine. It seems like a terrible trade. I either have headaches, or I cannot digest anything," I say.

We pull into the doctor's office, Crissy parks the car. "Do you want me to come with you or wait?" Crissy asks.

"Please go in with me. I am scared, Crissy," I say to her. I am terrified, actually. I do not know why but I have a sinking feeling in my gut.

Crissy smiles and holds my hand. "Everything is fine," Crissy says. Something about the way she looked at me scared me. Do I look that bad? I look at myself in the mirror on the visor. My color is terrible.

We go into the doctor's office. The nurse waves us back to the back. Crissy and I go straight back to a room. Another nurse comes in and hands me a cup. "You know the drill; we need to check everything per doctors orders," the nurse says.

I go into the bathroom and pee in a cup. I set it in the window and go back to the room. Another nurse comes in and takes a lot of blood. "Crissy, I know you get tired of doing this with me," I say to her.

"No, I do not. I want to do anything I can for you," Crissy says.

Crissy and I wait for about thirty minutes when Joshua comes into the room. "Ellie, I have some good news and some not-so-good news. You have a high platelet count. We will do some more tests tomorrow to figure out what is going on; you might should bring John with you," Josh says.

"Is that the good news or the bad news?" I ask him.

"That is the bad news. But, Ellie, you are pregnant," Josh says.

I sit in front of Josh and Crissy, stunned. "I thought I was not able to get pregnant. But, Josh, I am on the pill, and I take all these medicines that I was told would not... But, wait.... how is this possible?" I ask Josh.

"Ellie, I have no answer for that, but you are pregnant. We can do an ultrasound to see how far along, and you will need an OB. I will work with your OB to make sure you have everything you need while you are pregnant. We do need to figure out why your platelets are so high. Do you have an idea of which doctor you want to use for your pregnancy?" Josh asks.

"No, it is not something I have thought I would need. Can you recommend someone?" I ask.

"Yes, Connor Mitchel, he is down the hall. I will have him come to see you and John tomorrow when you come back. Ellie, this will not be easy. I know nothing has been for a while, but we can do this together," Josh says. I hug Josh. "Thank Josh," I say.

Crissy and I leave the doctor's office. I have to be back in the morning at ten. I sit down in the car. Crissy has not said anything yet. She knows I am worried. "Crissy, do you think John will be happy?" I ask her. "Ellie, I think John will be over the moon," Crissy says.

Chapter 14

FlashBack

John POV

Jeff and I stop at a small diner to get lunch. We stop at the same place every day because that is where Jeff wants to eat. We sit down and order the same blue plate special I have eaten every day for as long as Jeff has been my partner.

"You know there are other places we could eat lunch," I say.

Jeff rolls his eye. "I like it here," Jeff says. "Of course you do. You have had your eye on that waitress for as long as I can remember. If I get you her phone number, can we go somewhere else tomorrow?" I ask. "Don't you even think about it, young buck," Jeff says.

The waitress brings us the blue plate special. I take a bite of the sandwich when my mother comes into the diner. "John," she calls out to me. She comes over and takes a seat with Jeff and me. The waitress comes over and brings her a cup of coffee.

"Is Ellie okay?" I ask her.

My mother puts cream in her coffee. She looks as if she is trying to find the right thing to say. "Mother, is Ellie okay?" I ask again.

"Yes, Ellie is fine, but she did get some news at the doctor this morning. She is a little freaked out. She wanted to tell you herself, but she is so scared," My mother says.

I shift in my seat and take a deep breath. I swear I have a lump in my throat, and my heart is beating out of my chest. So why would Ellie be afraid to tell me anything?

"What did Josh tell her this morning?" I ask. I am almost afraid of the answer I am about to get from my mother.

"First, let me tell you her platelets are higher than they should be, and Josh is going to do some test tomorrow to find out why. This is not what she is worried about at all," my mother says.

"I can take off tomorrow and go with her if that is what she is worried about; it is not a problem," I say.

"John, listen to me carefully; she has an appointment in the morning at ten with Josh; there will be another doctor there to see her and talk to you also. I do not feel right being the one to tell you this, but Ellie is so upset that I volunteered to come to find you," my mother says.

"Mother, you are making me crazy; spill it already," I say.

"Well, John, it looks like you are going to be a daddy. Ellie is pregnant," my mother says.

I sit in the booth in the small diner, thinking about how scared Ellie is and how happy she is too. I want children, but we knew it probably would not be an option for us. I was not expecting ever to get this kind of news.

"John, are you okay?" my mother asks.

"Yes, take me to her now," I say.

"Go, young buck, go," Jeff says as I get up from the table to go see Ellie. As I walk out of the diner, I look at the waitress Jeff is admiring. "Hey, that old man over there wants your phone number," I say to her. I smile at Jeff as I go out the door. He will probably kill me.

My mother drives me home to see Ellie. When we pull up, Crissy is sitting on the porch waiting for us. I get out of the car and go onto the porch. "She is sick. At least we know why she has been having so much trouble eating and keeping down food," Crissy says.

"Thanks for going with her," I say. I hug my sister. "You are going to be a daddy. I am so happy for both of you," Crissy says. "Is she happy?" I ask. "I think she is worried, John. That is all. She is not very healthy, and this is scary for her," Crissy says.

I go into the house. Ellie is in the bathroom sick. I knock on the door. "Ellie, let me in so I can help you," I say through the door.

"I do not need help to throw up, John," she says.

I wait for her in the bedroom. She finally comes out and sits beside me on the bed. She leans her head over on my shoulder. "I love you, Ellie," I say to her. I put my arm around her and hold her.

"Are you happy?" I ask her. "Yes, John, I am beyond happy. I am so afraid that this is something that you do not want. I am scared, that is all," Ellie says.

"Ellie, I am so happy right now. I cannot tell you how happy this moment is for me, but I am also worried about your blood work. We can be happy and scared," I say to her.

"I know. I am sorry I asked your mom to find you. I could not wait until tonight to find out if you would be happy or mad," Ellie says.

"When have I ever gotten mad at you?" I ask her.

"Never, I do not think you ever have," Ellie answers me.

"This baby is a miracle. We will enjoy every moment of this miracle together," I say.

"Then tomorrow, you can take the throwing up part over because I am over it," Ellie says.

"Are you going to tell your parents?" I ask Ellie.

"Eventually, I will, but today is our day. I do not want to spoil it with whatever they will have to say," Ellie says.

I take her hand, and we go out on the porch with my mother and sister. They are waiting to see if Ellie is okay. Ellie is strong and independent, but at times she leans on my family and me for support. This moment is one of those times. I am so lucky to have three wonderful women in my life. This baby will have so much love no matter what Ellie's family says or does.

"Tomorrow, Josh and Dr. Mitchel will do an ultrasound to see how far along I am if both of you want to come," Ellie says to my mother and sister. My mother is delighted, and so is Crissy to be invited to be a part of the journey with us.

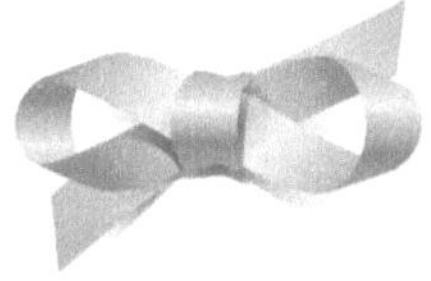

Chapter 15

I cannot seem to get it together this morning. I have to be at the doctor's at ten, and I am running so far behind. John got up early, cooked breakfast, fed my dogs, and cleaned the house. I hate that he is cleaning the house or cooking. He works so hard. He should not have to tend to me too.

"Ellie, I have you a cup of coffee and some toast ready," John says softly through the bathroom door.

"Oh, I do not think I can eat anything," I say to him. I splash water on my face and try to pull myself together. I dab on a bit of makeup and pull up my hair. I feel like I was run over by a truck last night.

I come out of the bathroom and go into the kitchen. John is eating his breakfast. The smell of the sausage he cooked turns my stomach. "Please never cook sausage again," I say.

"Ellie, I am sorry. I will go eat on the porch," John says.

"No, I will take my coffee outside. Open a window; I cannot take the smell," I say. He looks upset. I am not trying to hurt his feelings, and I only want to go five minutes without running to the bathroom.

I go outside with my dogs and drink my coffee. The cook breeze is relaxing as I sit on the porch and rock, drinking my coffee. I could sit here all day. Crissy and Missy pull up in the driveway.

Missy gets out of the car with a big bag. Please do not be any kind of smelly food. She rushes up on the porch and hands me the bag. "I brought you something," Missy, John's mother, says to me.

"Thanks, mom," I say to her as I open the bag. I look in the bag to find banana nut muffins. "I thought the muffins might go down easy," Missy says. Crissy rushes up behind her and sits down on the porch with me. "Where is John?" Crissy asks. "I left him in the house with the stinky kitchen," I say, laughing. "I will help him clean up the kitchen," Missy says as she goes into the house.

Crissy and I sit and eat the banana nut muffins. The muffins are divine. I think I could eat this every day. "Are you nervous?" Crissy asks me. "No, I am actually fine this morning. I had a meltdown last night, and now I am good. I think John is a bucket of nerves, but he will be okay. We have been here a thousand times. I am always sick. I hate that I am always bringing bad news to him, and it always turns out fine," I say.

"Well, yesterday, you brought the most amazing news," Crissy says.

"Yeah, I did. I think he is thrilled," I say to Crissy.

"I think you are right," Crissy says.

"I do worry. I cannot drive. I have health problems. How will I care for a baby?" I ask her.

"You have all of us to help you," Crissy says.

"I know that, but it is not fair that you and your mom always having to run over here and help me," I say.

"Trust me; we do not mind at all. We love you and John. This baby will have so much love from all of us," Crissy says.

"I know all of you will love the baby, but I have no idea what my family will say about this," I say.

"Their opinion does not matter. You and John are happy, and that is all that matters," Crissy says.

"You are right," I say.

John and Missy come out on the porch. John leans down and kisses me. "I can still smell the sausage," I say. "I could not stand the smell of bacon when I was pregnant. But, I promise it gets better," Missy says.

"When?" I ask. "Oh, in about nine months, give or take," Missy says. "Great," I say.

The four of us get into Crissy's car to go to the doctor's office. We stop several times so I can be sick. "This has to stop," I say. "I promise it does get better," Missy says.

We go into the doctor's office. John signs me in at the desk. I take a seat. I look around and think about how many times I have into this office a nervous wreck. I know Joshua and his nurse get sick of my calling all the time.

Samantha calls me back. Sam has been with Joshua for a few months, and we have become fast friends. As soon as the door closes to the lobby, she hugs me. "I was off yesterday, but I found out this morning. I am so excited for you," Sam says.

"We are all excited and nervous," I say. "Everything will be fine, Dr. Mitchel is a fabulous doctor, and he is easy on the eyes," Sam says with a laugh.

Sam takes us to a room with an ultrasound set up. "Okay, you will need to undress and put on this down. Dr. Newbern and Dr. Mitchel will be in here in just a second. Have you ever has an ultrasound?" Sam asks. "Yes, for an ovarian issue a few years ago," I answer. "Well, depending on how far along you are, we might see a baby today. Do you know when your last period was so I could figure out a due date for you to compare to the ultrasound?" Sam asks.

"Sam, I have not had a period in over a year," I say to her. "Okay, we have to rely on the ultrasound. I will let the doctors know you are ready for them," Sam says.

I go behind the screen and slip into the gown and get onto the table. John covers me with a sheet. "I am terrified," I say to him. "Nothing to be afraid of, my lover," John says.

Joshua and Dr. Mitchell come into the room. "I am going to let Dr. Mitchel do the ultrasound since that is his department, okay Ellie," Josh says. "Okay, that works for me," I say. Dr. Mitchel applies a sticky gel to my stomach and goes to work. He and Josh look at the screen and point at some things on the monitor.

"Ellie, when was your last period?" Dr. Mitchel asks.

"Over a year ago," I answer.

"Well, How long have you been sick in the morning?" he asks, still looking at the screen.

"Months, I really do not think it is related to the pregnancy. I have been sick at my stomach for probably over four-month," I answer.

"How about meds? Are you on a new med?" Dr. Mitchel asks.

"Yes, Josh can give you my list," I say.

Josh hands Dr. Mitchel my file. He looks over the meds. "Ellie, we are going to have to stop all of these meds and try something else. None of these are safe for a pregnant woman to take. I will go over your chart and collaborate with Josh on your meds," he says.

"Not safe. Is the baby okay?" I ask.

"Oh yeah, look here at this beautiful baby. Ellie, you are 14 weeks pregnant, and it looks like a girl. You are going to have to put on a little weight. I am concerned about that," Dr. Mitchel says.

"14 weeks, I was not expecting to be that far along," I say.

"You and baby girl looks great. I want to see you next week. Stop the meds. If you get a headache or become sick, call my office or Josh. I will call the pharmacy for you a prenatal vitamin to start immediately. I want you to try to put on a little weight, okay," Dr. Mitchel says.

"What about my platelet counts?" I ask.

"I am going to have some more blood work done today and set you up for some tests. Then, I will have my office call you about the tests," Dr. Mitchel says.

He shakes John's hand and leaves the room. Josh goes with him.

"What is twenty-six weeks from today? It is June 25th today; somebody gets a calendar," I say. Missy counts the weeks quickly on the calendar hanging up in the room.

"It is Christmas Eve; your baby is due on Christmas eve," Missy says.

"We are having a little girl, John, on Christmas," I say.

I see the worry on John's face. I go behind the screen and slip into my clothes. When I come out, I touch his face. "You know what, I will be fine. I have the three of you and this baby," I smile. I am happier than I have ever been in my life.

Chapter 16

FlashBack
	Ellie POV
Thanksgiving Day

It seems unreal how much weight I have managed to gain over the last few months. My blood work is terrific, and my headaches are almost nonexistent. Josh and Dr. Mitchel found a new medicine for me to try that seems to work well with me. As a result, I am able to drive and be more independent for the first time in years.

"John, today is the day. I am calling my mother," I say to him.

"Are you sure? What if it goes bad? I do not want you upset on the holiday," John says.

He is right about one thing, it will probably go wrong, but I want to do it. I want to call her and tell her about the baby. Leah will be here soon, and I want her to know. She is my mother, and I feel like I need her to be there for me.

"I need to do this," I say. John being the wonderful supportive husband he always is, kisses me on the forehead and smiles. "I support you no matter what," he says.

Crissy and Missy are busy cooking in the kitchen. We decided to have Thanksgiving here since I needed their help decorating the nursery. I wanted all of us to do it together. I go into the back bedroom, my old room, and now soon to be our precious Leah's room. I pick up the phone and dial the number. My heart sinks when the phone begins to ring.

My brother Thomas answers the phone. "Tommy! Happy Thanksgiving!" I say happily. "What you finally come to your senses, sister?" Thomas asks. "Can I speak to mother, please?" I ask. "Sure," he says and slams the phone down. We were once so close, and now he hates me.

My mother comes to the phone. "Hello, Ellie. If you are calling for money, the answer is no," she says as soon as she picks up the phone. "No, mom, I would never ask you for anything. I am calling because I have some news," I say. "Did you finally decide to come home?" my mother says. "John and I have been married for three years, get over it, but that is not why I am calling, but now I wish I would not have called. I called to tell you that I am pregnant," I scream into the phone.

Dead silence. I wait for a moment. "You have just killed yourself. You know the doctors said no children, Ellie. What have you done?" She says. I cannot take anymore, and I hang up the phone. I cry for a moment and then pull myself together. I put on a smile and go back to John.

John knows when he sees me that it did not go well, but he says nothing. Instead, he holds me and lets me cry for a moment. "I love you, Ellie," John says.

After a moment, his mother and Crissy come into the bedroom to check on me. "Everything okay?" Crissy asks.

"Yes, everything is perfect," I say. I put a smile on my face and kiss my husband. Then, the four of us go into the kitchen to finish cooking Thanksgiving dinner.

I sit at the table and look at the three of them laughing. I would love for my mother to love me like that. But, it will never be like that for my family and me. I will always give baby Leah love and understanding. I do not care who she marries as long as she is happy; if she wants to be an accountant or cashier, I will always support her as long as she is happy. I know that John and these two amazing women will too.

I touch my stomach, and baby Leah is kicking like crazy. "Come feel this," I say. The three of them place their hands on my abdomen as baby Leah dances around for them. "She is a showstopper," John says.

We sit down to eat. The meal is unbelievable. John fixes my plate for me. My feet are swollen from being on them all day, and he loves doting on me. "This is too much, John," I say. "No, you need to gain a little more weight," he says. "I have gained plenty. I am bigger than I have ever been in my life. I will never get rid of this weight," I say.

There is a knock at the door. "Did you invite Jeff?" I ask John. "I did, but he has plans with the blue plate special," John says, laughing. "You know she has a name," I say.

John goes to the door. It is silent for a few moments, and then screaming and shouting started pouring into the house from the porch. "What is going on out there?" I ask Missy and Crissy.

The two of them go to the door to see what is going on outside. Now four voices are screaming. Finally, I cannot take anymore. I go to see what is going on on the porch. When I open the door, I see Thomas and John screaming at one another and Missy and Crissy standing between them.

"What is going on?" I scream as I come out the door onto the porch.

Thomas charges at me. "What is wrong with you? You just had to call and upset mother today, didn't you?" Thomas screams at me. "Thomas, I only wanted to let her know that I am pregnant, " I say. "No, you always have to make everything about you, Ellie," Thomas continues to scream at me.

We go around in circles screaming at each other. Finally, I have had enough. "Thomas, I am done with you and them; please leave," I say to him. I walk past Thomas to go into the house. Thomas grabs my arm. "Wait, Ellie," he screams at me. John grabs Thomas. "Let her go," John yells at him.

John and Thomas start pushing and shoving one another with me right in the middle of them. "Stop, Please!" I plead with them. John lets go of Thomas, and Thomas rams right into me. I tumbled down the front steps onto the ground.

"Ellie," Everyone is screaming my name as I hit the hard ground stomach first.

Chapter 17

FlashBack
John POV

Ellie falls off the porch and lands her stomach first on the ground. I push past her idiot brother and run to her. There is blood on her head. I roll my precious wife over carefully. Her eyes are vacant. "What have you done?" I scream at Thomas.

Thomas kneels down beside Ellie. "I am so sorry, Ellie," Thomas says. He touches her. I push him off of her. My mother and Crissy come off the porch. "I will call an ambulance," My mother says.

I look at Thomas. I have so much hatred for him at this moment. I want to wrap my hands around his neck and choke the life out of him. "I did not mean for her to fall," Thomas says.

"You and your family have hurt her enough. Get out of here, now!" I scream at him. Thomas gets up and runs back to his car. He takes off before my mother gets back.

"This was not his fault. There was too much emotion and too many high tempers on the porch. I know he never meant to hurt her," Crissy says.

"Not now, Crissy, please, not now," I say to her.

My mother comes back outside and joins Crissy and me on the ground with Ellie. I keep talking to her, but she is not responding to me. This cannot be happening. "Oh, God!" My mother screams and begins to cry.

I look down and see blood pooling under Ellie. Her pants are soaked with blood. "Ellie, Ellie," I call to her, still no response.

The ambulance pulls into the driveway. I back away and let them work on Ellie. My mother answers all of their questions. I get into the back of the ambulance with her after she is put into the ambulance. My mother and Crissy follow us to the hospital.

On the way to the hospital, the EMTs start an IV and keep talking to her. Ellie does not respond to them or me. "Will she be okay?" I ask as we ride to the hospital. They keep working and do not answer me. I cannot lose her or baby Leah, not today.

When we arrive at the hospital, her doctor is there waiting for us. I get out of the ambulance. They take her back and take me to a waiting room. My mother and Crissy are already there waiting for me. "Dr. Mitchell came in and spoke to us, John. She and baby Leah are in great hands," My mother says.

Ellie is only back a few minutes when Josh comes into the waiting room to talk to me. "I saw Ellie and Dr. Mitchell. They are doing an emergency c-section, John. As soon as I know something, I will be back to let you know," Josh says.

I hang my head in my hands. My mother and Crissy sit with me as I cry. I cannot believe such a good day turned so sour. All Ellie wanted was to share her fantastic news with her mother and look at what happened. But then, just when I think things could not get any worse, I look up to see Thomas coming into the waiting room.

"How is she?" Thomas asks.

I do not look up at him. Instead, I look at my sister. "Crissy, get him out of here now, or I will kill him," I say calmly to my sister.

Crissy gets up and takes Thomas by the arms. She leads him out of the waiting area and out of the hospital. I hate what he has done. He had to show up and make everything about him.

Hours pass for us, waiting for news on Ellie. "John, everything is fine. They are working on her. Josh will be back soon to let you know how things went," My mother says.

I can tell by the look in her eyes she is worried too. Ellie does not deserve this. She wanted a nice family dinner and then for us to work on Leah's room as a family. That is all she wanted, a family day.

I look up to see Josh standing at the door. "John, I need you and your family to come with me," Josh says.

We get up and walk out of the hospital waiting area and down the hall to a small office. Josh waits for us to sit down, and then he sits down in front of me. "Ellie is recovering and awake. She will be in a room soon. The baby is in the NICU. But, John, I am going to be real honest with you. It does not look good," Josh says.

"How soon can we see both of them?" I ask.

"I can take you to see your daughter now. You cannot hold her, but you can see her. She looks a little rough, and she has a lot of tubes. I am only warning you before you go up to see her. You can see Ellie in about an hour. I will go with you to see baby Leah, and then I can walk you up to see Ellie," Josh says.

"Can we come?" My mother asks.

"Yes, but only John can go into the NICU. You can look at her through the window," Josh says.

The three of us follow Josh to the NICU to see baby Leah. I feel like I am dragging my heart behind me as I walk up to the NICU. I cannot imagine how Ellie feels. Her baby was taken from her, and she cannot even hold her yet.

We approach the nursery. "Crissy, Missy, there she is right there," Josh points to this tiny baby in through the window.

"She is only a little early. What is going on with her?" My mother asks.

"Several things are going on with baby Leah. But, even if she would not have had such a dramatic entrance into the world, we would still be here," Josh says.

"She is a fighter like Ellie, and she will be fine, John," Crissy says.

I go into the NICU. They suit me up in a mask and gown. I follow Josh back to her incubator. I look down at the most beautiful little baby I have ever seen in my life. I cannot believe this tiny being belongs to Ellie and me.

"You can put your hand throw that little hole and touch her if you want," Josh says.

"It does not seem fair for me to see her before Ellie," I say. "I do not think Ellie will mind at all," Josh says.

I slip my hand through the little hole on the incubator and touch her hand. I am so in love with this little being. I never knew my heart could feel this full. "You are strong, little one," I say to her.

Chapter 18

"John," I try to call to him, but only a whisper comes out of me. My entire body hurts. "John, John," I call out, pushing as much air out of my body to make a louder voice to get his attention.

He finally hears me and rushes to my side. He places his hand on my forehead and brushes my hair, his other hand touching my hand and holding it tightly. "Ellie, you are awake," John says.

"How is she?" I ask him, still whispering.

"She is the most beautiful little being I have ever seen. She looks just like you. She is tiny; oh Ellie, she is so tiny," John says.

Ellie smiles. "Am I okay?" Ellie asks. "Yes, Dr. Mitchell said you would be very sore from the c-section, but you did great. Unfortunately, you have a mild concussion, but you are fine," John says.

"Where is Thomas?" I ask John. His face turns to anger then he smiles at me. "He came to the hospital, but I sent him home," John says.

"It was not his fault. I should not have got in between the two of you. I should not have gone on the porch," I say.

"This is not acceptable. He should not have come to our home acting the way he did. What if something would have happened to you or Leah?" John says.

"My brother is an asshole, but I do not think he was trying to hurt Leah or me," I say.

"What do you want me to do, Ellie?" John asks.

I pat his hand gently. "Call Thomas for me. I want to see him," I say to John.

"You are asking a lot of me, Ellie. I want to beat his ass, and you want me to call him and ask him to come to see you," John says.

"For me, please," I say.

"Okay, my love," John says. He kisses my forehead. I know he disagrees with me, but I do not want Thomas thinking this is his fault. Thomas is an asshole, but we were close once upon a time. I do not want any bad blood between us, even if we never speak again.

John leaves to call Thomas for me. Crissy and Missy come in to see me. "Ellie, we saw baby Leah from the window. She is beautiful," Missy says.

"Yes, she is a beautiful little baby," Crissy says.

"I cannot wait to see her. Hopefully soon," I say.

"You will, soon," Crissy says.

"Where did John go?" Missy asks.

"I asked him to call Thomas. I want to speak with him about what happened," I say.

"He was broken up pretty bad, but John was furious with him. Ellie, you cannot blame John for being upset, but I understand that Thomas is your brother, and you want to mend fences. What about your mother?" Missy says.

I shift in the bed. "I am not ready for that discussion, but I am sure that my mother is done with me," I say to her.

They do not understand. They are a close family. My family hates me. I chose to be with John, and they cannot live with my choice. My family decided I do not exist anymore. I wanted my mother to know about her grandchild, and she does not care.

John comes back into the room. "I talked to Thomas. He is on his way to see you, and your mother is coming with him," John says.

I want to smile and be happy, but I know it will not be a happy reunion. I am sure she will find a way to make everything that happened John's fault. But, in reality, it is mine. John will never blame me for what happened on the porch, but I know it is my fault.

"When they get here, I want to talk to them alone, John," I say to him.

The three of them look at each other. I know they are concerned. John is always concerned for me. I hate that he has to worry about me so much. Now, in reality, our focus should only be on baby Leah and nothing else. I will mend this fence the best I can with my family and then let it go for John and our family.

As we sit waiting for my brother and mother to make their entrance, there is a knock on the door. John's mood changes immediately. He becomes defensive and moves closer to me. "Come in," I say.

A tiny woman comes through the door. "Daniella Bradley?" She asks.

"Yes, that is me, but everyone calls me Ellie," I say. "I am Dr. Angela, and no one can pronounce my last name, so we will leave it at that. I am the doctor seeing Leah Bradley," she says.

"We can wait outside," Crissy says, taking Missy by the arm to lead her out.

"No, stay, please," I say to them.

"How is Leah?" John asks.

Dr. Angela comes in close to me. "Daniella, I am sorry, Ellie, your daughter, has some issues. She will not a lot of care after she leaves the hospital. I want to make sure you have everything you need for her. I will set you with a specialist to help you with her, and you will probably need a nurse. Has anyone explained to you her diagnosis?" Dr. Angela says.

"No, I have not even seen her yet," Ellie says.

"Well, then we need to get you up and moving so you can see your beautiful baby girl," Dr. Angela says.

"Dr. Angela, please tell me what is going on with Leah?" I ask.

"Ellie, she has a Congenital heart defect and Down syndrome," Dr. Angela says.

"Will she live?" John asks bluntly.

"What baby Ellie has is in the left side of her heart; it is too small and did not develop properly. She will need surgery soon," Dr. Angela says.

"Is this fatal?" John asks again.

"It can be, but I cannot say for sure. It all depends on her," Dr. Angela says.

John puts his strong arms around me and holds me. "I want to see my baby," I say.

"I will have a nurse come help you out of this bed so that you can see your baby, Ellie. Then, I am going to consult with a specialist for baby Leah, and we will talk some more," Dr. Angela says.

As Dr. Angela leaves the room, my brother and mother stand outside my room in the hall. They walk into my hospital room with a chip on their shoulder.

"Why are you so upset?" My mother asks me.

"Leah is sick," I say. It is all I can get out. "Of course she is; you knew better than to do this," My mother says. Thomas shakes his head.

"Leave, both of you need just to leave," John says to them.

"She wanted to see us, John. I guess she wanted to invite us to the pity party," My mother says.

"No, I wanted to talk to Thomas. I did not want him to feel at fault for what happened," I say.

"Of course, he does not feel at fault, my dear. You fell off the porch. You should have been more careful," My mother says.

"Why? Why do you hate me so much?" I ask her.

"I do not hate you, Daniella. I hate your choices," My mother says.

"Leave now, or I will make you leave," John barks at my mother.

I cry into John's shoulder as my mother and brother leave. "I am sorry, John. I should have listened to you," I say, crying.

Chapter 19

John POV

Flashback

Watching those people who call Ellie family hurt her is too much for me. I do not want them around her or Leah. I will fight for my family with everything I have in me. I do not need these people upsetting Ellie. It is not a wonder she spent her life sick. If I had to live with that horrible woman, I would be sick too.

After calming Ellie and helping her into a housecoat mom bought for her in the hospital's gift shop, she finally is out of bed and in a wheelchair. Ellie will finally get to see baby Leah. I feel terrible I was able to touch baby Leah and lay eyes on her before Ellie. She deserved to be the first person.

The nurse lets me push the wheelchair, and she follows along behind us. My mother and Crissy stay behind this time. They want Ellie to have her moment with baby Leah. Why couldn't Ellie be blessed with family like me? It is a wonder Ellie is as kind as she is after being raised by those horrible people. Ellie is one of a kind, a gentle soul.

When we get to the NICU, Ellie is wheeled in first, and I stay behind and watch through the window. I see Dr. Angela coming as I watch Ellie finally meet our baby girl. "John, she looks so happy," Dr. Angela says, watching Ellie with me.

"Yes, she is going to be a wonderful mother," I say. I cannot help but smile endlessly, watching Ellie. Her face is lit up as she finally sees her baby.

"John, we need to talk," Dr. Angela says.

"Ellie will be out in a minute, and we can talk," I say.

"John, I know Ellie has been through a lot, and I want her to be prepared for what is to come with baby Leah," Dr. Angela says.

"Ellie is strong; she can handle it," I say.

"John, I have no doubt Ellie can handle motherhood, but can she handle the worst-case scenario," Dr. Angela says.

I stand watching Ellie with baby Leah through the window. I think about what would happen if we lost baby Leah. "I do not know how to answer that. I hope I never have to find out," I say.

"John, the type of heart condition baby Leah has, is almost always fatal. I did not want to answer that earlier, but the truth is, and John listens up, I want to be frank with you here, the prognosis is not good for baby Leah. So take her home, enjoy that baby, but be prepared and prepare Ellie," Dr. Angela says.

"You and Josh think this news is better coming from me rather than a doctor?" I ask.

"Yes, I am not trying to hide anything from Ellie, but I feel like it is best coming from you. You know what, maybe Leah will be a miracle baby and shock us all," Dr. Angela says.

Dr. Angela pats me on the back and takes a look at Leah and Ellie, then walks away. I have no idea how I will break this to Ellie. She will be crushed into a million pieces. But, then again, maybe baby Leah will be a miracle. Could we catch a break and our baby live?

The nurse waves me in to see baby Leah. My heart is sinking as I go in, carrying this knowledge with me. When should I tell her? I go in and join Ellie and baby Leah. I put my arm around my wife. She has tears coming down her face as she holds baby Leah's tiny hand.

"She is so perfect, John," Ellie says.

I pull her as close to me as I can. "She is perfect," I say to Ellie.

One week later, I take Ellie home, but not baby Leah. Baby Leah will not be able to go home for at least another month. Ellie does not want to leave her behind, but she needs to go home and rest.

Ellie cries the entire way home. I try to comfort her, but she is inconsolable. When we get home, I help her into the house. We are not home five minutes when there is a knock on the door.

I settle Ellie in to rest in the bed before I answer the door. I go to the door, and it is Thomas. "What do you want?" I ask.

"I only want to see if they are okay?" Thomas says. "Ellie is fine, but Leah is still in the hospital," I say as calmly as I can. "I am sorry about how mom acted at the hospital," Thomas says. "Thomas, I have to tend to Ellie. Do you need anything else?" I ask him. "No, I am sorry, John," Thomas says. I slam the door in his face. Ellie does not need this right now.

Before I can even get back to Ellie, the phone is ringing. I stop in the kitchen to answer the phone. "Hello," I say. "Mr. Bradley, this is Dr. Angela; there is a problem with Leah; we need you both as fast as you can get her," Dr. Angela. "We are on our way," I say. I hang up the phone.

"Ellie, we have to go to the hospital now," I say to her. So Ellie gets out of the bed, and we leave immediately for the hospital.

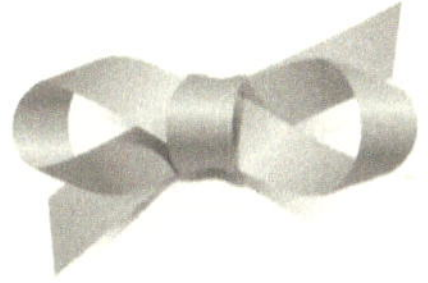

Chapter 20

Flashback
Ellie POV

John is so tender and sweet to me on the ride home. I know he is having a hard time, too, with leaving baby Leah behind. Crissy and Missy agreed to take shifts, so there is always family with her, but I feel like my heart has been pulled out of me and stomped.

John helps me out of the truck and into the house. I hear someone at the door, but John ignores it until he gets me settled. I want to lay down and sleep in my own bed for a few hours before we go back to see baby Leah. He leaves me for only a second. I hear him talking, and then the door slams hard. It had to be my family. I should have never told them about baby Leah.

John makes his way back to me. I hear him making coffee, and then the phone rings. John is on the phone for a split second and then in our bedroom. "Ellie, we have to go to the hospital now," he says as he helps me out of bed.

"What is the matter?" I ask him as he helps me out the door. "Dr. Angela wants us back now," John says.

The drive to the hospital is chaotic. John is driving like a madman. "John, slow down," I say as calmly as I can. He keeps driving crazy trying to get to the hospital. I touch his leg, trying to comfort him. Finally, he slows down and takes my hand. His eyes are filled with tears.

"We will get there in time," I say.

"Don't talk like that; she will be fine," John says.

John is on edge. I know there is no way for me to comfort him, so I stop trying. I just keep holding his hand. He pulls into the hospital, parks as close as he can. He comes around to help me out of the truck. We go into the hospital and move as quickly as possible to the elevator.

We get off the elevator and make our way to the NICU. Missy, Crissy, and Joshua are waiting for us. This cannot be good. "I should not have agreed to leave," I say to John. I am furious with myself. "You needed rest," John says calmly.

Dr. Angela rushes over to us. Missy, Crissy, and Joshua are all crying. "Mr. And Mrs. Bradley, you need to go in and see baby Leah. Her time is near. Her heart has failed her," Dr. Angela says.

John and I go into the NICU. "I want to hold her, John. I want to hold my baby, now!" I yell. The nurse comes over to me. "Mrs. Bradley, we are taking her out for you and your husband to hold. Do you want your family in here? She will pass soon," the nurse says to me.

I shake my head yes. "Go get your mother and Crissy; ask Joshua if he wants to come in too," I say calmly.

The nurse takes me to a small room. I look around at the pale room. Is this where they bring parents to say goodbye to their children? I try not to cry. The nurse comes back with baby Leah. John is behind her as she comes in the door to the small room.

"Do you want to hold her?" she asks John. "Ellie first," John says.

Missy, Crissy, and Joshua come into the room as the nurse places baby Leah in my arms. "When she stops breathing, send someone to let us know," the nurse says.

"How long does she have?" John asks.

"It is hard to say," the nurse says.

I touch her tiny face and kiss her cheeks. I hold her close and cry. I will never let her go, not ever. John kneels beside me. He kisses her head. "I cannot let her go, John," I say to him.

"I know, and that is okay Ellie," John says.

Missy and Crissy kneel with John so they can see her out of the incubator. I am selfish. I should let them hold her while she is alive. I take a deep breath and hand her to John. "I would hate myself if I did not let everyone hold her at least once," I say as I place baby Leah in her father's arms.

John takes Leah and pulls her so close to him. His face is wet from tears as he tells her he loves her. John would be the best father. But, unfortunately, I have robbed him of this opportunity. I hate myself for taking this from him.

Missy sobs as John stands to allow her to hold baby Leah. Missy and Crissy both hold her together. Joshua stands close to them to see her as well. Crissy takes Missy and brings her back to me. "She should be in her mother's arms," Crissy says.

The nurse comes back to check on us. She peeks in and sees us holding baby Leah, but she is still breathing and resting peacefully in my arms. Dr. Angela comes in next to check on baby Leah. She looks her over, still in my arms.

"She is so beautiful," Dr. Angela says.

"Yes, she is perfect and beautiful," I say.

For three hours, I hold her, and she sleeps peacefully in my arms. Finally, John takes her in his arms. He talks to her and tells her how much he loves her. John kisses her on the forehead, and then she takes her last breath in his arms.

Joshua checks baby Leah and nods his head. I know she is gone. He leaves the room to let the nurse and Dr. Angela know that baby Leah has passed. I sit stunned and devastated. I cannot move, or cry or even feel anything.

Dr. Angela comes back with Joshua to take baby Leah away. Missy goes with the nurse and Dr. Angela. I sit in the chair with no baby, numb. I want to die and be with her.

John and I sit in the tiny pale room for what seems like forever. "I should take you home," John says to me. I stand and follow him like a zombie. I do not speak. He tries to console me, but I push him away. "Don't touch me," I say. I walk alone ahead of him, crying. When we get to the truck, he opens the door for me. I get into the truck; he shuts the door and goes around to get in the truck.

I look at him. He loves me so much, and I hate myself for all of this. "Divorce me, John, so you can have a family," I say to him. John looks at me, angry. This is the first time he has ever looked at me angrily. "Don't you ever say anything like that to me again, Ellie! How dare you hurt me like that? What the hell! I am hurting too. We need each other, and I will be damned if you get to hurt me. Stop it!" John screams at me.

John has never raised his voice at me or spoke to me in anger. He begins to wail and sob loudly. "I love you, dammit!" He screams.

I lean over on him and cry with him. He holds me as we both let out our cries, screams, anger, and every pent-up emotion we have at the moment.

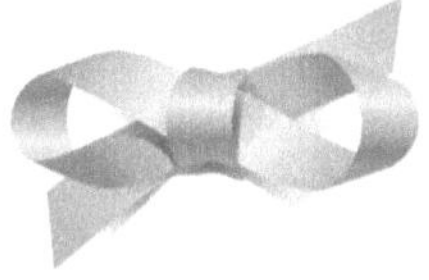

Chapter 21

Flashback
John POV

Ellie will not get out of bed. She sobs constantly. She refuses to see the doctor or take any medication she needs for her health. She is grieving, and I have no idea how to help her. Josh recommended a psychiatrist for her, but she refuses to see anyone.

My mother and sister will be here today to help me bathe her and dress her for Leah's funeral. Ellie is lost after losing baby Leah. I am too, but I have to continue to fight for Ellie. I know she feels responsible, but she is not to blame for baby Leah.

Ellie's mother came to see her, which only made things worse. I should have never let that bitch into the house. Why I did is beyond me? I thought she would comfort Ellie, but all she did was make it worse. Her mother, the bitch was telling Ellie how she should have known better than to try to have a family. Stella left Ellie screaming and crying. I hate Stella. The woman causes me to have emotions I did not even know I was capable of having.

I make myself a cup of coffee and continue to ponder all of the events over the last few days. But, Ellie, my precious love, I cannot let you fall into this deep depression. Please come back to me.

I do not hear my mother and sister come into the house. They walk into the kitchen and sit down at the table with me. We are all heartbroken and defeated.

"How is Ellie today?" Crissy asks me.

"She is still in the bed. I will let her grieve for now, but we will have to get her out of bed soon. Maybe after the funeral, she will start to heal," I say.

"Let her grieve, John. She needs to grieve. You need to grieve too," My Mother says to me.

"I will let her grieve, but not at the cost of destroying herself. She wants to lay down and die. I will not let her do that," I say.

My mother reaches across the table and takes my hand. "We will all help with Ellie, we love her, but I will not watch her destroy herself either," My mother says. Crissy nods her head in agreement.

We go into the bedroom to try to help Ellie out of bed. "Ellie, we need to get you dressed for the funeral," Crissy says to her. "Why did we agree to do this? We should not have agreed to a damn funeral. I do not want to do this!" Ellie says.

I look at my mother. "Ellie, people are coming to be supportive of you and John today. Let everyone help you through this horrible time in both of your lives," My mother says.

I leave the room to let Crissy and my mother handle Ellie. Maybe they can calm her down. We have barely spoken since we left the hospital. I know I cannot calm her right now. I love her, and I will fight for our marriage. She hurt me badly with the horrible words she spoke to me, but I forgive her. When life settles down, I will talk to her and make things right between us. For today, I only want to get through burying our child.

After an hour, the three women emerge from the bedroom. Ellie is dressed and moving like a zombie. The four of us walk to the car in silence. Ellie cries to the vehicle, in the car, and getting out of the vehicle. She cannot be consoled no matter what we do for her.

We get out of the car at the funeral home. The amount of people that have shown up to say goodbye with us is massive. Jeff and several officers are here, along with my captain. As we walk into the funeral home, there is no one from Ellie's family. Not a single person from her family came to say goodbye to Leah.

Ellie looks around the room. I know she is looking for her mother, but she did not come. I am glad we opted for only a quick service and no viewing. I do not think Ellie could handle sitting there with baby Leah and wondering why for hours.

The priest kept the service very brief as instructed. We walked together to the cemetery beside the church to lay baby Leah to rest. Ellie walks slowly and still not speaking to anyone. She is inside herself, and no one, not even I, can pull her out of that dark hole she is in right now.

The graveside service is also brief. I try to hold her hand and comfort Ellie, but there is no consoling a mother that blames herself for her child's death. None of this is her fault. After this day, I hope that I can convince her to talk to someone about how she feels. We both need support from others and not turn on one another. I will not let her turn into something bitter.

Ellie stands next to baby Leah's grave as everyone leaves the gravesite. She looks at the hole in the ground and the dirt surrounding the tiny hole in the earth. "Ellie, you do not have to stay and watch this part," I say to her.

Ellie shakes, and her lip quivers. "I have to stay until this is over. I have to watch to know it is real," Ellie says.

Watching her so broken is too much for me; I walk to a nearby tree and sit down underneath it to wait for Ellie. My mother joins me, and Crissy stays with Ellie.

"John, she will come back to you, but it will take time. You have to be her rock and son. I know that leaves a burden on you to have to carry, but you have to do it. Do not forget to grieve yourself; you cannot hold this pain inside you either," my mother says to me. She sits down beside me under the tree. Poor Crissy has to watch baby Leah being buried. I hate that for her. I cannot watch. I do not want to see the dirt going onto the tiny pink coffin that holds the most precious creature in the world.

Chapter 22

P resent Day
     John POV

Ellie screams as we run to her. She has been in so much pain the last few days. Maybe Joshua was right, and I should have convinced her to stay in the hospital longer. I know she did not want to die there. She wanted to come home and be with her dogs and us when she dies.

I take her hand and hold the rough hand that once was so soft. "Ellie, I am here for you," I say softly. She opens her eyes. "I saw her, I saw our baby girl," Ellie says, crying. I begin to cry. I look at my mother and sister, who are sobbing.

There is a knocking on the door. "Whoever it is, get rid of them," I say to my mother. "No, please do not leave me," Ellie says, grabbing my mothers' hand. The knocking continues as we sit with Ellie. Ellie closes her eyes for a moment.

Crissy steps back, crying. She steps out of the sunroom to sob. I hear Crissy go to the door and scream at someone. It has to be Ellie's family. I am not leaving Ellie, and they are not welcome here. I do not want them near her right now.

Ellie begins to scream again. "I am in so much pain," Ellie screams. "Get her some morphine," I say to my mother. "She already had her morphine, John," My mother says. The words break as she tries to sympathize with Ellie.

"Someone call Joshua now," I say. "Do not leave me, please do not leave me," Ellie cries, holding my hand tightly.

Ellie closes her eyes and drifts into sleep again, tears still rolling down her face. "Go call Josh, please, and check on Crissy," I whisper to my mother. She nods and leaves me alone with Ellie.

"She is here, John. Baby Leah is here with me," Ellie whispers. She is dreaming of baby Leah. She has dreamed of her so many times since we lost baby Leah. It is one of the hardest things for me to endure. I hate seeing her awake from a dream to only cry from seeing her. She has never stopped grieving the loss of our child.

My mother comes back in the room, "Josh needs to speak with you. I will hold her hand while you talk to him," my mother says softly. I leave Ellie with my mother to go into the kitchen to speak with Joshua.

I pick up the phone. "Josh," I say.

"John, I can come over if you like or if Ellie needs me. I can be there in ten minutes," he says.

"She is in pain, Josh," I say.

"I am on my way. Do not give her any more pain medicine until I get there," Josh says.

"Understood," I say.

Crissy grabs me as I walk back to be with Ellie. "Thomas is here asking to see Ellie," Crissy says.

"Tell Thomas to go to hell," I say as I walk away. I will be damned if he is going to upset her today. To hell with him and her family.

My mother looks terrified when I go back into the sunroom. Ellie is so pale. Her once beautiful skin now pale; she looks blueish against her pink gown. "She is having trouble breathing, John," My mother says.

"Josh is on his way, now," I say.

I take Ellie's hand. I am trying so hard to be strong for her. She screams again and then closes her eyes again. "She needs something for pain, now. She cannot wait on Josh," I say, crying.

"John, you cannot give her anything else; it might..." My mother says.

"It might what? Kill her! She is dying already in case no one has noticed," I cry out.

Josh comes into the house and runs back to the sunroom where we are with Ellie. Josh looks at Ellie and the three of us. Ellie opens her eyes and sees Josh. "Joshua, my friend," she says softly, then screams out and closes her eyes again.

"John, I can give her more morphine, but she will die if I do," Josh says.

I shake my head and cry. "Do it; make the pain stop. I cannot stand for her to be in any more pain, " I say.

My mother gets the box that contains Ellie's meds and hands Josh the morphine. Josh fills a syringe full of morphine and injects Ellie. Ellie looks up at me, touches my face, and kisses at me. "I love you so much," Ellie says. I lean down and kiss her lips. Ellie closes her eyes and takes in her last breath.

As I hold her hand, sobbing, Thomas comes into the house. I have had it with this today. I let go of Ellie's hand and rush into the living room where he is standing.

"Please let me see her; I only want to apologize for everything," Thomas says.

"She is dead," I scream at him. I grab Thomas and drag him out of the house. I throw him off the porch. "You killed her. You had to come up here and push her when she was pregnant. The cancer did not kill her, you bastard. Ellie died from a broken heart that you caused. You and your mother killed her. She did not deserve any of this," I scream!

"I never meant for any of that to happen. I was wrong for coming up here that day. I have played it over and over in my head a million times. I blame myself for Leah's death," Thomas says.

I run off the porch and jump on him. I start hitting him. I cannot stop myself. Josh comes out of the house to try to stop me from killing Thomas. I feel Josh pull me off of him. "This is not what Ellie would want," Josh says. I brush myself off. "Thomas, I do not want ever to hear

Leah or Ellie's name uttered from your lips again," I say as I go back into the house.

I go back to the sunroom and sit with Ellie. My heart is gone. Baby Leah and Ellie are gone. I have nothing left to live for anymore. I want to be with them.

Crissy comes to me. She sits with me. "I called her nurse and the funeral home for you," Crissy says. I try to thank her, but no words can escape my mouth. Why? I do not understand why?

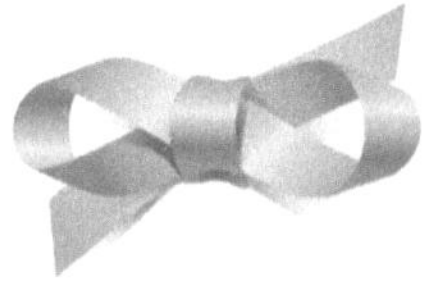

Chapter 23

F lashBack
    Ellie POV

John goes back to work only a week after baby Leah is buried. I try hard to pull myself together for him and for myself. But, I just cannot find it in my soul to get out of the bed.

I know he is frustrated with me. I am just tired and hurting. My body hurts, my soul aches, and my heart is shattered into a million pieces. I do not want to talk to him about how I feel or anyone else for that matter. He wants me to go to this stupid group for people who have lost a child. I will not go. I do not want to be in a room with other people in pain. I want to stay home and emerge myself in my own pain, no one else's.

When he left this morning, he kissed me and told me he loved me. I know he loves me more than he loves himself. I have to find a way to bring myself out of this but not yet. I am not ready.

I sit on the side of the bed. I should get up. I should shower and eat, but I cannot bring myself to move. I lay back in the bed and cover myself with my comforter and cry myself to sleep.

I awake to a beating on the door. No what! Probably someone else is coming by to drop off food or come in to see me. I do not want to see anyone. The knocking persists. I finally drag myself out of bed and put on a robe. I go to the door and open it.

John's captain is at the door. I take a deep breath and open it. "Hello Steven," I say. "Ellie, get dressed and come with me," Steven says.

"NO, I am not going anywhere," I say to him.

"Ellie, It is John; get dressed and come with me," Steven says to me. This time he is more demanding.

I rush back to the bedroom and grab the first thing I come to in the drawer. I put on pants and a shirt. Then, I grab my shoes and run out to the porch to meet Steven.

I pull my hair up and slip on my shoes in the car. "What happened?" I ask.

"Ellie, John was shot. He is in surgery. I tried to call you, but you did not answer," Steven says calmly.

"I did not want to talk to anyone. I guess I should have answered the phone," I say.

"I called Missy. I told her I would pick you up and for her to go to the hospital," Steven says.

Steven puts on his sirens and rushes me through traffic to the hospital. I have experienced enough heartache at this hospital. We pull in, and he stops at the emergency room entrance.

"Jeff is in there waiting for you; go, Ellie," Steven says.

I get out of the police car and run through the entrance. I look around for Jeff. I am starting to panic when Jeff comes up behind me. "Ellie, follow me," Jeff says.

"What happened?" I ask.

"It was the craziest thing. We were called to a domestic call. John tried to defuse the situation. Finally, everyone seemed to have calmed down, and then the husband shot John and then himself," Jeff says.

"Have you talked to anyone since he got here?" I ask.

"They took him straight up to surgery a little while ago. I don't know anything. I will stay with you if that is okay," Jeff says.

Jeff takes me to a waiting room. Crissy and Missy come into the waiting room after Jeff, and I sit down. The three of them sit with me for hours, waiting for some news on John.

Finally, a doctor comes into the waiting room to talk to us about John. "Mrs. Bradley, your husband, is in recovery," he says.

"Will he be okay?" I ask.

"Yes, you can see him if you like. I will have a nurse walk you up to his room," the doctor says.

The three of us walk up to John's room with a nurse. As I walk behind her to see John, all I can think is I have been so vicious to him. He lost baby Leah too. I have to tell him how sorry I am for how I have been acting toward him.

We go into John's room. He is not awake. He has a lot of tubes and wires coming out of him. He looks swollen. I touch his strong hand and lean over to kiss him softly. "I love you, John," I whisper to him.

Crissy and Missy gather around him. Jeff stands back. I can tell Jeff is worried. To see someone like Jeff worried makes me anxious about John. We sit with John for at least an hour before he finally opens his eyes. I smile the biggest smile at him.

"That smile looks good on you," John says in a whisper.

"How do you feel?" I ask him.

"I feel sore and like I was shot," John says.

"Well, young buck, I am happy to see you are okay," Jeff barks at John.

I touch his face and smile. I cannot stop smiling at him. "I will stay with you," I say to him.

"No, you need to rest. I will be fine here," John says.

"I am not leaving you, John, ever," I say to him.

"Promise me you will never leave me," John says.

Everyone in the room thinks this is a tender moment between us, but in truth, I know he has been worried I would pack and leave.

"Nothing will ever separate us, I promise," I say to him.

Chapter 24

John POV

I sit with Ellie's lifeless body waiting for the funeral home to come to take her away from me. I feel a strange sense of relief for her. All the pain is over for her. The heartache of losing a child, the pain of being sick, and the constant worry that she is a burden.

Ellie worried for others and how they felt more than anyone I have ever met in my life. Her pain was enormous, and so was her love for people and animals. Ellie was like no other.

After I came home from the hospital from being shot, Ellie took care of me better than I ever have taken care of her. I sit here looking at her, and all I can think is, did I give her the same level of care she gave me. First, she bathed me and fed me until I was back on my feet. Then, I let her wait on me, which I would have never done if I would not have been so sore from the wound. She enjoyed being the caretaker for a change, and it kept her mind off of baby Leah for a while.

I think the hardest thing for Ellie was the day I went back to work after the incident. She was afraid of losing me, and she was scared of being in the house alone. That is when we went from two dogs to six dogs. She needed someone to need her and depend on her.

Ellie made it clear she never wanted to be pregnant again. Finally, after a lot of debate, she talked me into agreeing to get her tubes tied. She never wanted to experience the heartache of losing a child again. It was always her decision. I decided because she needed me to agree with her. She needed someone else to say it is okay to give up on having children. I never wanted her to feel that pain again.

Fate had other plans for Ellie and me, and that is the one shocker that I think pushed Ellie to be where we are today, without her. The day Ellie went to talk to Dr. Mitchell, her life took a drastic turn and put her in a horrible mental state that she never recovered from until her heart beat for the last time.

Flashback

Ellie is waiting for me when I get off work. She is sitting on the porch looking like she is completely lost in herself again. I sit down beside her and notice her face is wet.

"What is wrong, Ellie?" I ask her.

"I went to see Dr. Mitchell today about having my tubes tied, and he agreed to do it, but first, he needed to do a pregnancy test to make sure I am not pregnant. Then he would schedule the surgery," Ellie says.

"Are you having second thoughts? If you are worried about the surgery, then I can get clipped," I say, smiling, hoping to put her in a better mood.

"No, that is not the problem," Ellie says. Tears begin rolling down her face, and she sobs loudly, then screams.

I am mortified at what is going on with her at the moment. I have never seen her like this except for the day we buried baby Leah.

"Ellie," I whisper softly and kneel in front of her.

"John, he did the test and then some blood work and then did a freaking ultrasound," Ellie sobs.

She is shaking her head violently. "Ellie, calm down and tell me what is wrong," I say calmly, placing my hands on her upper arms, trying to console her.

"I am pregnant again, John," Ellie says.

I am stunned. I would love for this to be a happy moment for Ellie and me, but it is sheer horror for her. I pull her close to me and hold her tiny body. She has lost so much weight since baby Leah passed away.

"Tell me what you want me to say or do. I know you are not happy, but I do not know how to help you right now," I say to her.

"That is just it, John. I am happy. I am okay with this. Is that wrong? I do not want our baby to think we will forget her," Ellie says.

"No, my love, she would want you to be happy. I want you to be happy. I love you," I say.

Ellie seems to calm down and stops crying. She finally smiles at me. "I know you hate that I am this way. I try so hard not to be so dramatic, but it is who I am," Ellie says.

"Have you told anyone yet?" I ask her.

"No, not yet. I wanted to have my meltdown with you first, and then we can tell Missy and Crissy," Ellie says.

"I am off tomorrow. So we can have them over and tell them. I think it will make them happy to see you happy again," I say to her.

Ellie and I go into the house to cook dinner together, as we do almost every night. We listen to the radio and dance in the kitchen. I have not seen her this relaxed and happy in a long time.

"You must be superman," Ellie says, joking.

"What does that mean?" I ask her.

"Because you have barely touched me since your accident. We use to make love every night, and now I need an appointment. Yet, you still managed to get me pregnant, so yes, superman," she says.

"I am sorry that I have not touched you or tried to make love to you. You were so sad, and I was in so much pain, but we are getting back to normal," I say to her.

"Yes, we are getting back to normal. I feel good. I have not had any headaches or problems in a while. So maybe I am normal again," Ellie says.

"You are perfect. You are dramatic, but perfect... and beautiful... and sexy... and I want you now," I say to Ellie. I kiss her in a way I have not kissed her in a while. Not since the night, she came to me wanting to be held and wanting me. I left her alone to grieve, and then when she became my caretaker, she wanted me again, and I wanted her.

It has been a slow process. I feel guilty for wanting to be with her. I know I should not, but I wait for her to make a move every time I want to be with her. I do not want to push her away, but I never meant to make her feel like I did not want her.

I carry Ellie's tiny body to bed and lay her on the bed. I remove my shirt and pants before I get in the bed beside her. I lay beside her. I let my hand run over her beautiful body, removing her shirt and shorts. I lean down and kiss her as I touch her. There is nothing sexier than her right now, beside me on the bed looking at me so in love and wanting me.

I slide my hand into her panties and begin to pleasure her as I kiss her. Ellie tilts her head back and moves her hips. Tonight feels so different. It feels like we are normal again. We are us.

I kiss her breast and grind against her. I want her so bad I can not breathe. She makes my body ache to be inside her. She pulls me close to her, and before I can make a move to make love to her, she has me on my back and mounts me.

Ellie is on top of me, rocking her hips and taking me inside her. She is hot, sexy, and so beautiful on top of me. She is in charge, and I love it. I move my hands down to her bum and grip on tight to her. I push up into her, and she moans with pleasure.

Ellie pushes down on me, she takes my hands, and we hold hands as she releases her warmth onto me. We change positions so I can take her. I slide into her deeply, pushing in and out of her to please her again. I kiss her lips, then her neck, penetrating her deeper.

Ellie rolls her hips under me, sending me into a euphoric state of pleasure. I begin to release my seed into her. I lean down and kiss her. I want this moment to last forever—Ellie and I in love with each other and happy.

Nothing lasts forever. We did not make it through the night happy. But Ellie was delighted after we made love. We held each other for hours. Then she gets up to go to the bathroom and comes out crying. "I am bleeding, John," she exclaims.

We dress quickly and go straight to the emergency room. Ellie lost the baby. That was it for her. Her happiness was gone; our happiness was snatched from us so quickly. Ellie cried for days. We were back to square one, Ellie in the bed crying nonstop, blaming herself. This time I decided to do something and made her an appointment to see a mental health doctor.

Again, life slapped us in the face. Not only did Ellie lose the baby, but the very next week, we got a call from Dr. Mitchell. Some of Ellie's tests were back, and it did not look good. Ellie is sick again. This time we know what is wrong with her, cancer.

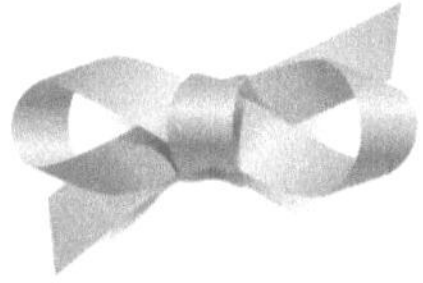

Chapter 25

John POV

I am going through Ellie's closet like a madman. I cannot focus. My mother comes into the bedroom to try to help. "John, what are you doing?" my mother asks.

"I am looking for the yellow dress that Ellie loved so much. The one with the white flowers on it. I always told her she looked like a sunflower in it. I want that dress," I say.

My mother pushes me out of the way and takes the dress out of the closet. "Is this it?" my mother asks.

"Yes, thank you," I say.

"Do you want me to drop the dress off for you?" My mother asks.

"I can do it," I say.

"Do you want me to clean the sunroom or the house or anything?" my mother asks.

"No, I took some time off, and I will need something to do. Nothing like putting my house back together to be alone," I say.

"You are not alone," my mother says to me.

"I feel alone. I miss her every damn second. I do not know how I will get through this life without her," I cry.

"You will get through it one sunset at a time," my mother says.

"That is what that damn mental health doctor told Ellie after she miscarried. One sunset at a time, Ellie. It infuriated her so bad that she swallowed a bottle of pills," I cry.

"John! You never told me that; when was this?" my mother asks.

I lay the dress down. The sweet scent of Ellie coming from the dress is maddening to me.

"I promised her I would never tell anyone. Josh came over and gave her something to make her throw it all up. We kept it quiet for her sake. Ellie was never the same after she miscarried. I think she was relieved when she found out she had cancer. You know she was almost herself when she found out she was pregnant. She was so happy that night. We danced and talked that night. We felt like we were close again. We were almost there. Losing Leah and then a miscarriage... Ellie wanted to die," I say.

"Ellie loves you and wanted to live for you," my mother says.

"Ellie loved me, not loves; Ellie is gone," I cry.

"Pull yourself together, John Bradley, now!" my mother says to me.

"I can't. I need time to work through all of this," I say.

"John, I want you to do something for me. First, I want you to say goodbye to Ellie and Leah. Then, I want you to get it all out, and then I want you to live. I want you to live your life. I am not trying to be hard or heartless, but I will not put you in the ground, too," my mother says.

"I will, mother, I promise. I will live for them," I say.

My mother hugs me tightly. "You will live for yourself, son. You were a great husband, and you loved that baby. You have sacrificed everything, even your own grief. I want you to grieve and find a way to live after this is over," my mother says.

She is tough, and I know why. She is afraid I will barricade myself in this house and never leave again. She knows how much I love Ellie. I love her, not loved her. I will love her until the die I die.

"I have to take the dress to the funeral home," I say, picking up the dress.

"Let me do it, and you work on the sunroom. Keep your mind occupied, and I will be back with something to eat with Crissy. John, you tired as I have never seen a man trying to find a reason for her to live, but Ellie was lost after Leah died and then the miscarriage. It was a lot of grief for one person to handle. She loved you, son. She just could not figure out how to live after losing Leah. Never second guess her love for you, never. She was flame in the fire, and eventually, flames burn out," My mother says.

My mother leaves with the yellow dress for Ellie. I have asked too much of her. At least she is present for Ellie, which is more than I can say for her family. They were only present when it suited them. I am happy I found Ellie and that I shared my family with her.

Flashback

I come into the house, and it is quiet. Ellie had an appointment with the mental health doctor today. I hoped she would feel like herself today, but the house is quiet and dark.

I put down my things and go into the bedroom. She is asleep. I kiss her on the cheek. She is holding a note. I pick up the letter and take it into the kitchen.

** I love you, but I cannot live one sunset at a time. I want to be with my baby **

Damn! I run back to the bedroom and try to wake Ellie. She opens her eyes. "What did you do?" I ask her.

I look at the bottle on the bedside table, and it is empty—damn sleeping pills. So I grab the phone and call Joshua.

"Ellie swallowed a bottle of sleeping pills!" I scream into the phone. "I am on my way," Josh says.

I pull Ellie close to me. "Josh is on his way, and we will get you to the hospital, Ellie," I cry into her.

"No, hospital. Let me die," she whispers.

"I cannot live without you. You promised never to leave me, Ellie. You promised we would navigate life together," I cry.

Josh comes into the house. He comes straight back to the bedroom. He examines her and checks the bottle. "I just wrote this prescription a few days ago," Josh says.

Josh goes into his bag and takes out a syringe with liquid in it. "Hold her mouth," Josh says. I hold Ellie's mouth open, and Josh forces the liquid into her mouth. Ellie tries to spit it out, but she is too weak.

Josh puts the second syringe of dark liquid into her mouth and holds her mouth shut.

"She is going to throw up all night, and I will stay to make sure it all comes up unless you want to take her to the hospital. I know she does not need this on her medical record or her family to get wind of it," Josh says.

"I only want her to be okay, Josh. You are her doctor; you tell me what we need to do," I say.

Ellie begins to throw up. I carry her to the bathroom to hold her over the toilet. I wipe her mouth and clean her face as the sleeping pills exit her body.

"Why do you love me so much?" she whispers to me.

"You are dramatic, hard-headed, beautiful, sexy, but most important, you are the love of my life," I say to her.

"I do not want to go back to that damn doctor. He is making me relive Leah, and I cannot do it anymore, please John, either let me die or do not make me go back there," Ellie says.

I sit on the cold bathroom floor, holding her limp body. I brush her wet hair out of her face. "Just don't leave me and never do this shit again," I say to her.

Ellie throws up most of the night. Finally, she falls asleep at daybreak. Josh and I are both exhausted from caring for her all night. He loves her like a sister. He is the only family she has besides mine.

I lay Ellie in the bed and go into the kitchen to make coffee. "I will only give you her prescriptions going forward. She needs help, John," Josh says.

"I will figure out something to help her," I say.

"John, Ellie is very sick; we both know that she is sick, but this is not the way out. She needs help," Josh says.

"I know. I am here with her every day, watching her die piece by piece," I say.

"John, her cancer is progressive, but she could beat it if she fights. Unfortunately, I do not believe Ellie has any fight left in here. She is refusing every treatment offered to her. Did she tell you that? She wants to die, John. We cannot let her give up," Josh says.

"Ellie gave up a long time ago, Josh," I say.

"Then help her find a way to live again," Josh says.

Josh leaves me alone in the house with Ellie. I have to find a way to make her want to live one sunset at a time. I just do not know how, but for her, I will figure it out.

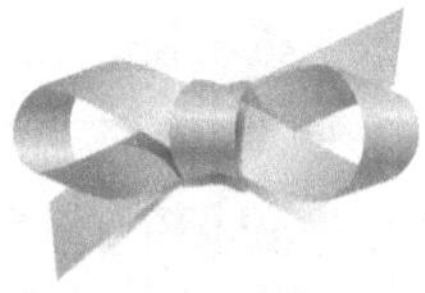

Chapter 26

John POV

Crissy and my mother arrive at the house to drive me to the funeral home. It is time to say goodbye to Ellie. I have tried to be strong and be the man Ellie would have wanted me to be today, but I am tired. I am not ready to deal with everyone at the funeral home, but I know that these people loved Ellie.

We ride silently on the drive to the funeral, and I am thankful for that. I am not ready to talk about how I feel. My mother is fully aware of how I feel, and so is Crissy. I don't think I should have to say it out loud.

When we arrive at the funeral, Jeff is waiting for me outside. He is smoking a cigarette and looks worried. The rough older man had a special place for Ellie. I am thankful he pushed me when I needed it. He has been there so many times for me over the years. To say I am grateful to him would be an understatement.

I get out of the car and walk over to Jeff. I do not see the blue plate special with him, and I do not ask where she is today. He hates when I pry into his business.

"Young buck, I am sorry about Ellie. She was a special lady. Everyone loved her," Jeff says to me.

"Yes, she was a special lady, Jeff," I respond.

My mother and Crissy join me. We walk in with Jeff. "A lot of people are here already, and they got here early to see you, John. Everyone is worried about you, even me. So if you need anything, well, you know," Jeff says.

I walk into the funeral home, and so many people begin to come up to me with hugs and to say they are sorry. It becomes overwhelming fast. I know they mean well, but it is a lot to handle on this day. Jeff stays close to me, and I hate to admit how much I need him right now. I think he knew I needed him.

The funeral director comes to collect my mother, Crissy, and me to going first with Ellie. I am dreading this moment. I do not want to see her or remember her like this, but I know I have to do it. I have so much to say to her before I bury her. I want her to know how much she is loved and how hard I tried for her.

We enter the room to see Ellie. The room is cold and smells of flowers. The amount of flowers in the room is unbelievable. I think every person in town sent her flowers. I walk around looking at the flowers, slowly making my way to Ellie. I am trying to get my nerves together first.

"You can do it, John. I am right here with you," My mother says to me, taking my hand and leading me to the coffin containing the love of my life, my wife, my Ellie.

Ellie wanted a pink and white coffin adorned with white and yellow roses. She looks like a ray of sunshine, just sleeping in her coffin. The coldness of her hand in mine as I try to hold it is shocking to my soul. I feel my heart shatter as I look over my sunflower lying in her coffin.

"Whenever you are ready, we will let everyone into the room," Ross, the funeral home director, says to me. I nod to let him know I heard him and continue holding Ellie's cold hand. She is so frail. Her dress that she once filled out so perfectly does not fit on her as well as it did, but they tried to make it look like it did. Maybe I should have bought her a new one, but she loved this dress. I wanted her to wear the dress she loves. She wedding ring is sliding off her finger. It is so loose from her weight loss. I touch her ring and think of the day I put this on her finger. It makes me smile for a moment. Oh my, Ellie, how I have loved you forever and will love you forever.

"John," my mother says softly, touching my arm. "I know, mother, I need to let everyone in to see her," I say in a whisper.

I sit in a chair next to her pink and white coffin as the funeral director opens the door for people to come into the room to say their goodbyes to Ellie. It seems like an endless parade of I am so sorry, John, to the point I feel like running away from here and not looking back. If my mother, Crissy, and Jeff were not here, I probably would run. Ellie would hate this. She would hate such a big fuss over her. She never liked being the center of attention.

People parade in and out for over an hour. We finally wrap it up, so we can have her graveside service. Ellie would hate all of this. I choose to do this so people could say goodbye to her. I tried to think of others and not myself. Although right now, I wish this was over. I wish I would have thought of myself and only had the graveside service.

Everyone leaves the room so that I can say my goodbye to Ellie before the graveside service. "I want to be alone with her," I say. My mother, Crissy, and Jeff leave the room to give me a moment with her. A moment is all I have left with the love of my life, and a moment is not enough time to say goodbye to her.

"I do not know how to say goodbye to you, Ellie. I loved you. I still love you. Death will not change the amount of love I have for you or your flame. Mom said you were a flame in the fire and that it was your time to burn out. I cannot accept that. I cannot accept that your time had to be so soon. If you are a flame in the fire, then I want to be your flame too. Two flames in the fire burning together for eternity. I tried to give you a reason to live, but I know losing Leah and then being in so much pain was just too much for you. I hope I gave you as much love as you gave me. I hope you carry that with you in the afterlife. I will see you soon, wait for me, goodbye Ellie," I say to her. I kiss her on the forehead and walk out of the room.

Also by Lillith Mykals Kennedy

The Vampire Authority
The Auction

Standalone
Dirty Little Secret
Flames In The Fire
Her Obsession